Disenchanted
Princess

More delicious reads from Simon Pulse

The Private series
KATE BRIAN

The Mob Princess series
TODD STRASSER

The Fashion-Forward Adventures of Imogene series
LISA BARHAM

Bloom
ELIZABETH SCOTT

Two-way Street
LAUREN BARNHOLDT

The Social Climber's Guide to High School
ROBYN SCHNEIDER

Disenchanted Princess

JULIE LINKER

Simon Pulse

NEW YORK LONDON TORONTO SYDNEY

SIMON PULSE

An imprint of Simon & Schuster Children's Publishing Division

1230 Avenue of the Americas, New York, NY 10020

Copyright © 2007 by Julie Linker

SIMON PULSE and colophon are registered trademarks
of Simon & Schuster, Inc.

Designed by Mike Rosamilia

The text of this book was set in Cochin.

Manufactured in the United States of America

First Simon Pulse edition July 2007

2 4 6 8 10 9 7 5 3 1

Library of Congress Control Number 2007920202

ISBN-13: 978-1-4169-3472-1

ISBN-10: 1-4169-3472-3

To Mama. Thank you.
For everything.
I love you.

And to Annabelle, my baby princess.
I love you more than you'll ever know.

ACKNOWLEDGMENTS

My unending gratitude to Lauren Barnholdt for setting all this in motion. Lauren, you rock.

My sincere thanks to Nadia Cornier who, in addition to being the hippest agent around, sold this book incredibly quickly and never complains when I act like a needy, insecure writer.

A great big thank-you to Jennifer Klonsky, the best editor EVER. Jennifer, I'm afraid I'm spoiled forever now.

Kathia, this whole writing thing wouldn't be nearly as fun without you. Thank you from the bottom of my heart.

To my family—Candice, Carolyn, Ryan, Daddy, and Ona—thank you for always being supportive of me (even when you have no idea what I'm talking about). And to Bob, who will never get to read this book, but who I know is looking down from heaven. Thank you for always being proud of me.

I would also like to thank Amy Bell for offering to share her seat that day five years ago and for being my very first "editor." Amy, I'm so glad we're friends. Thanks also to Heather Wyatt-McCreary, who has championed me ever since the snack-cake incident when we were seven years old. Heather, nothing in this book is based on our school experiences, but I'm not making any promises about the next one. . . .

And last, but most definitely not least, I would like to thank my husband, Gary, who has always taken my writing seriously and doesn't care that I have zero domestic qualities. Without his support, I could never have seen this dream to fruition. Thank you, baby.

One final thing—to the many, many teachers who reprimanded me for reading novels during class—I lied. I was never sorry. And I'm still not.

1

My Forced Exile into the Land of Hillbillies, or: Proof That God Hates Me

"I'm never going to see you again!" I cry, clutching Maria's arm in a death grip. I'm making a scene in the middle of LAX, but I don't care. My whole life is falling apart, and this is my last chance to salvage some of the pieces.

"That's not true," Maria says firmly, trying unsuccessfully to disengage herself from my clutches. "Your father will fix this. You have to be strong."

Be strong? I'm being shipped off to the middle of nowhere and all she can say is "Be strong"? Next she'll be comforting me with something really helpful, like "When life hands you lemons, make lemonade."

I let go of her arm and grab a big handful of her shirt. "Please let me stay, please, please, pleeeeease."

Unfortunately, Maria expected something like this, which is why she brought José, our gardener, along. Even though he devotes most of his life to growing flowers, José is the type of guy you wouldn't want to meet in a dark alley. He's massively built, and you can tell he probably got the hideous scar on his left cheek from a knife fight or some other equally scary thing. I'd love to know the whole story, but nobody in their right mind would dare ask him about it. He's THAT scary.

José steps forward, his face as hard as granite. *"No más,"* he says forcefully, removing my hands as if they were twigs. *"Vas a perder tu vuelo."* José always speaks Spanish, even though Maria says he can speak English fluently. That's probably true too, because the time I accidentally got the gas and brake pedals mixed up and drove Daddy's new Mercedes into the wall of the garage, José said "fuck" perfectly, without an accent or anything.

"Last call for Flight 1725 to Little Rock," a woman's voice says over the loudspeaker.

José pushes my candy-colored Louis V into my hands and steers me toward the security checkpoint. I look back pitifully at Maria, the only mother I've ever known. My biological mother died in a plane crash when I was a baby. She was a really famous fashion model, and her plane went down on the way to a photo shoot in the Bahamas.

That sounds like a made-up story, I know, but it's totally not. Really. There's an *E! True Hollywood Story* about her and everything—"Crystal Kendall: Tragic Beauty."

Maria says it's good I was so little when she died because that way I don't remember her. Maria's mother died when she was twelve, and it still really bothers her. Sometimes she even wakes up at night calling out for her and saying things in Spanish I can't understand.

Except the weird thing is that I DO remember my mother. I mean, intellectually, I know that I don't *really* remember her, but I've spent so much time reading articles about her and looking at her pictures that sometimes it seems like I do. It's like I've constructed this whole imaginary person in my head. Crazy, huh?

"I love you," I tell Maria, holding back the sobs that are threatening to overtake my body.

"*Vamos,*" she says, shooing me toward the gate. Tears are rolling down her face, ruining the MAC foundation and blush I picked out for her last week at Saks. I try to go back to her, but José steps in front of me, an impenetrable fortress. I have no choice but to go through the gate.

I hoist my Louis V higher on my shoulder. All right, if I'm going to have to go through with this nightmare, I'm going to do it with dignity. Like the time I had to go to an Orlando Bloom premiere with green hair because I had gone swimming too soon after my highlights. A lot of people would have bailed, but I just put my hair in a messy topknot, threw on a cute little Galliano and some funky earrings, and went with it. It was a risk, but it paid off. Joan Rivers pronounced it "the most fashion-forward look she'd seen all year," and I even got a tiny pic in *Teen Vogue*. I mean, surely if I can pull off green hair, I can pull this off.

Lifting my chin, I walk forward through the gate like I own it. Arkansas, here I come. *Yee-haw.*

2
The 411 on Me

Okay, so you're probably wondering why I'm being exiled from L.A., though if you read the papers, you probably already know a little about my situation. Oh, except I didn't tell you my name did, I? My bad. I'm West Deschanel, daughter of Jean-Claude Deschanel, the supersuccessful Hollywood agent who was recently convicted (wrongfully—he was totally framed) of embezzling money from his clients. And instead of just letting him pay a fine (which would have been no big deal because we're totally rich), the judge sentenced him to FIVE YEARS in prison.

I mean, come on, that's a little harsh, don't you think? It's not like he was plotting terrorist activities in our basement or anything. And to make it even more awful, he is SO innocent. His slimy accountant Neal totally framed him. I knew from the start that guy was bad news. I mean, who trusts a guy named *Neal*?

Anyway, with my dad in prison and my mom dead, that left me an orphan, legally speaking. Of course, I was a filthy rich orphan, so it's not like anyone felt sorry for me or anything. Plus, I still had Maria. Daddy's lawyer, Luke, drew up the papers to make her my legal guardian, but in a soap opera-ish twist of fate, the day before everything was finalized, a woman with big hair and a Southern accent came into the house all gangbusters and announced that SHE should be my legal guardian, not Maria.

Okay, so technically she buzzed the intercom at the end of the security gate and dropped her little bombshell during lattes and low-fat chocolate chip cookies with Maria, but it's the same difference. She TOTALLY screwed up my life.

Miss Big Hair turned out to be Sherri Reynolds, my mother's younger sister, who had come to L.A. to announce that she wanted me to live with her. On a farm. In Arkansas.

Naturally, I freaked out because (A) living on a farm in Arkansas is number nonexistent on my list of cool things to do before I die; and (B) my "Aunt Sherri" is the weirdo who sends me a pair of gloves and a package of Hanes Her Way underwear every year for Christmas.

Need I continue? I mean, B alone is proof the woman is an unfit guardian. I relaxed, though, because Luke PROMISED me there was no way the judge would award custody to anybody but Maria. Except he SO lied, which just proves you can't trust anyone, even if they work at the biggest law firm in L.A. and wear custom-made Versace.

The judge turned out to be one of those "blood is thicker

than water" types who thought it would be good for me to "get to know my roots." I told her that I pay Andre, my hairdresser, very good money to make sure I *don't* know my roots, thank you very much, but she said she didn't care. Actually, her precise words were "Don't get cute with me," but I took that to mean the same thing. Then she proceeded to give me this big, long lecture on how she was tired of all these "entitled" teenagers and how she could send me to some juvenile detention center if I didn't do what she said.

Um, can you say power trip? It was SO obvious that she's just one of these cranky middle-aged women who hate anybody younger and prettier than they are. I pointed out to Luke the blatant green monster on her shoulder, but he said that wasn't a valid legal argument. I assumed he had some other fancy legal maneuver up his sleeve, but no. Mr. nine-hundred-dollars-an-hour was done. And to make matters worse, Luke said she was totally telling the truth about the detention center thing.

So. Here I am on my way to—are you ready for this?— *Possum Grape*, Arkansas. That's right, you heard me. Possum Grape. My dear auntie lives in a town named after a rodent and a fruit. And that horrid judge is trying to make me live there too. But I can't. I won't. I mean, I know I'm on this plane and everything, but I refuse to be beaten by a woman who wears a black tablecloth to work every day. She may have won the battle, as they say, but this war is FAR from over.

Uh-oh. I'm getting myself worked up and I'm supposed to be trying to cultivate inner peace. I've been dabbling in

Buddhism, and let me tell you—Buddhists are ALL about inner peace.

I close my eyes and try to focus on my breathing the way I learned in my Buddhist meditation class, but this annoying jingle from a Diet Coke commercial keeps intruding on my thoughts. Great. Now I'm thirsty. I crane my head over the back of my seat and motion to the entirely too perky guy who's my flight attendant. He bobs happily up the aisle and promises to return in a few seconds with a bottle of Evian.

As I turn back around I accidentally look directly into the gaze of the man sitting next to me. Uh-oh. I cut my eyes away immediately, but it's already too late. He sticks out his hand. "Hi, I'm Ted," he says in a low, husky voice he obviously thinks is sexy, but makes me want to gag into my air-sickness bag. First of all, he's forty-ish, which means he's the same age as my dad. Second, he's been openly staring at my breasts ever since we got on the plane. And third, he's wearing a fake Rolex.

I look at his hand as if it's the most revolting thing I've ever seen and make no move to take it. His smile disappears when he realizes I'm not going to suddenly pull him into the bathroom and make him a member of the Mile High Club. Disgusted, he pulls his hand away and mutters, "Sheesh, I was just trying to be friendly."

Yeah, right. I shoot him a look to clue him in that I know he's full of it. Men like Ted only have one thing on their minds and, trust me, it's not making friends. I know this because I deal with it a lot. Hollywood is full of older men trying to catch a little action with girls young enough to be their daughters or, in some cases, granddaughters. Or in one really, really dis-gusting incident, their great-granddaughter, but I don't want to talk about that or else I'll really have to use my air-sickness bag.

I used to try to be nice to guys like Ted because I didn't want to hurt their feelings, but I've learned from experience that you can't give them one iota of encouragement. Zero, zip—not even shake their hand. It's better to just be a total bitch from the start.

The flight attendant reappears with my water. Ted immedi-ately asks him for a screwdriver, even though it's, like, nine in the morning. Good. Maybe he'll keep drinking them and pass out, so he can't stare at my breasts anymore.

I uncap the water and take a long swallow, then settle back in my seat as I mentally construct an imaginary wall between me and Ted. Okay, where was I? Oh yeah, my breathing. I close my eyes and try to start again, but the same freaking Diet Coke commercial starts playing in my head.

I open my eyes. All right. Maybe I should just forget about my breathing and think positive thoughts instead. Arielle, my life coach, says it's important to visualize good things happen-ing because it makes them more likely to come true. It really works too, because last month I could NOT find a dress for this super-important charity event (I mean, I went *everywhere*), so I finally tried visualizing myself finding the perfect outfit, and the very next day I found the most fabulous Chloé dress you ever saw.

So, maybe if I visualize positive things about this whole

Arkansas thing, I'll find another fabulous Chloé dress. Not literally, of course, but you know what I mean. So let's see, good thoughts, good thoughts . . . I know! I'll think about what my aunt's house is going to look like. House stuff is totally fun.

I snuggle farther down in my seat and start mapping it out. It'll be one of those huge, white Southern mansions, with Greek pillars and a big front porch, sort of like Tara in *Gone with the Wind*. There'll be a crystal chandelier in the entryway, and an elegantly curved staircase. For the SHORT time I'm there, I'll spend lazy afternoons sitting on the front porch exchanging witty banter with my eccentric yet brilliant Southern friends.

We'll laugh and discuss Mark Twain and Tennessee Williams, and a maid in a crisp black-and-white uniform will bring us mint juleps. I'm not exactly sure what a mint julep has in it (mint obviously), but it sounds yummy, don't you think? The house will be surrounded by majestic oak trees and fields dotted with sleek horses . . . my eyes fly open.

Horses! Of course! Why didn't I think of them earlier? If I'm going to be forced to go to this place, I might as well make the most of it, and I've wanted to learn to ride ever since I saw this awesome black-and-white layout of Jacqueline Kennedy and her horse. She looked so refined in these black breeches with a fitted jacket and a smart little whip. I totally want an outfit like that.

Forgetting all about my positive thinking, I lean forward and dig through my bag for my sketchbook. When I finally find it, I have to flip through a ton of pages to find a blank one because I've almost completely filled the whole thing up. Designing is my passion—have I mentioned that yet? I'm going to be a famous fashion designer. I used to say I "wanted" to be a famous fashion designer, but Arielle says it's better to say "I am" so that you eliminate the possibility of failure from your mind. Isn't she, like, so totally smart?

Anyway, designing is part of the reason why I have to get back to L.A. ASAP. You see, my best friend, Delaney, and I are throwing our annual end-of-summer party in just TWO WEEKS. Our blowout this year is fashion themed, featuring my original designs. We're going to have a mini fashion show with a catwalk and models and everything. And, more impor-tant, Zane Porter is going to be there.

In case you've been living under a rock, Zane Porter is the hot, new, straight (gasp!) twenty-something designer who has recently taken L.A. by storm. Pssst. You want to know a little dish? Yours truly is dating him!

Okay, so a string of random club hookups isn't exactly *dat-ing*, but we also text each other practically every day. Besides, I wouldn't want to be with him exclusively or anything. Hello, I'm only sixteen. I'm not about to tie myself down with some-body, even if he did dress Reese Witherspoon for the Oscars.

Anyway, Zane has no idea I'm a designer too, but I'm going to surprise him at the party. And once he sees how talented I am, he'll totally want to take me on as his intern next summer. That's why getting back to L.A. in time for the party is SO important. Being Zane's intern next summer is a crucial step in my plan to debut at New York Fashion Week when I'm nineteen.

I know what you're thinking: Why am I in such a hurry

when I have my whole life ahead of me? Frank, my therapist, recently told me it's because I'm secretly scared I'll die young like my mother, so I'm trying to cram everything in just in case. And my only response to that is . . . hello? He's just now figuring this out? I have a therapist, a life coach, AND a Buddhist meditation teacher. Do I seem like somebody who is just coasting through their teenage years?

Anyway, a lot of people think I'm going to go into modeling or acting because of Daddy's connections and my looks, but I'm so over the whole actress/model thing. All of Daddy's girlfriends are actresses/models and they are SO lame. The only things they talk about are their trainers and their stupid auditions.

And even though Daddy hasn't been in a single long-term relationship since my mom died, they all think they're going to marry him and be the next Mrs. Jean-Claude Deschanel. That is so not going to happen. Daddy says he won't ever marry again because my mother was the love of his life, and nothing could compare to that. Isn't that so romantic and tragic? It's just like Kate Winslet and Leonardo DiCaprio in *Titanic*— except for the whole sinking ocean liner thing.

I work diligently on my new sketches until the vibration of the plane's engines makes it hard to keep my eyes open. We didn't have time to stop at Starbucks for my usual caffeine fix, so I'm operating on less steam than usual.

Tucking my sketchpad and pencil back in my bag, I lean back against the seat and close my eyes. I feel a lot better about everything after all my positive thinking. I mean, after all, how bad can Arkansas be?

3

Tara: The White-Trash Version

This is not happening to me, this is not happening to me, this is not happening to me. . . . I close my eyes and repeat this mantra over and over again, but when I peek through my lashes (which are lusciously thick, thanks to the two coats of Chanel mascara I applied before de-boarding), the awful people are still standing in front of me.

And by awful, I mean completely, totally, and appallingly deficient in all the important categories: grooming, fashion, and cosmetic dentistry.

Sherri comes toward me, her hair even bigger than in L.A., her arms outstretched. "Welcome home, Caroline!" she squeals, crushing me to her chest. I cringe and not just because she's wearing some sort of hideous perfume.

First of all, Caroline is my middle name and I don't go by

it, so I have no idea why she's calling me that. Second, this place is NOT my home, and I don't care to be welcomed to it like some sort of prodigal daughter or something.

"Thanks for picking me up," I gasp when she finally lets go of me.

C'mon, you didn't think I was going to do the whole spoiled, sulky teenager thing, did you? I'd like to, of course, but I have to extricate myself from this situation, and, as the saying goes, you get more flies with honey. I mean, mint juleps and curving staircases are great and all, but I'm getting out of this place.

Sherri smiles at me, revealing the reason teeth whitener was invented. "Of course we came to pick you up, hon. You're family." She turns and motions to the people behind her. "Y'all come on up here so I can introduce you to Caroline."

Why is she calling me that? I wonder as the people shuffle forward reluctantly. Actually, there aren't as many of them as I first thought, just a man and two kids, a boy about my age, and a little girl who's probably six or seven. Sherri's family, I assume. I know she has a couple of kids, because that was another reason why the judge said it would be good for me to live here. She said having pseudo-siblings would be an "enriching" experience. Whatever. I could have just gotten a dog.

I put on my best fake smile, hoping they hadn't noticed my horrified expression when I first saw them. By rights I shouldn't be worried about hurting their feelings since Sherri isn't worried about RUINING MY LIFE, but I can't help it. My upbringing won't allow me to be openly rude. Damn Maria. If only she'd been inattentive and uncaring like all my friends' nannies instead of smothering me with love and drilling good manners into my head, I could totally be channeling Naomi Campbell right now.

"This is your uncle Joe," Sherri says, pulling on the man's arm until she's maneuvered him in front of me.

Uncle Joe? I don't even know this guy. Does she really expect me to call him that? Does she expect me to call her *Aunt* Sherri too?

My first reaction is no way, but then I remember the fly and honey thing. I sigh inwardly. All right, all right. I'll call them Aunt and Uncle. I'll call them anything they want if it'll help me get back to L.A.

I force myself to act enthusiastic. "Hi, Uncle Joe," I say brightly, sticking out my hand. I have to crane my neck to look him in the face because he is really, really tall, probably about six feet four. He's also really, really thin, and his face is severely sun damaged. Haven't these people ever heard of skin cancer? I have the urge to offer him some of my moisturizer with SPF, but I resist the temptation, considering we just met, like, two seconds ago.

We shake, and he mumbles something unintelligible before dropping my hand really quickly like he's afraid I have a communicable disease or something.

Next up is Clint, Joe and Sherri's son. Physically, he appears to be about my age, but fashion-wise he looks like a ten-year-old whose mom got him dressed that morning. His light blue, short-sleeved, button-up shirt is neatly tucked into his high-waisted blue jeans, which are secured by a braided leather belt and creased so sharply, they're probably dangerous. That's right, CREASED. I can practically see Sherri standing over them with a steaming iron. To make matters worse, he's also a little pudgy and has his hair buzzed to his scalp as if he recently signed up for the military.

I finger my cell phone inside my purse, tempted. Carson Kressley's number is in my address book, and if anybody ever needed a professional makeover, it's this guy. I know *Queer Eye* got canceled and all, but maybe they'd consider doing a reunion show. But again, there's that whole met-two-seconds-ago thing, so I guess arranging a makeover by famous homosexuals would be a little bit presumptuous.

Appearance aside, though, he's still around my age, so surely we'll have something in common, right?

I give him my best smile. "Hey, Clint. How are you?"

Displaying the same winning charm as his father, Clint stares at the floor with his hands crammed in his pockets.

"Say hello, Clinty," Sherri says, prodding him.

Clinty? OMG. Forget Carson Kressley. This guy is beyond help.

"Hey," he mutters, never lifting his eyes from the top of his seriously ugly boots.

Ouch. Strike two. The famous Deschanel charm apparently has no power south of the Mason-Dixon Line.

I naturally assume the little girl will be strike three, but when Sherri introduces Clint's little sister, Dakota, she immediately plasters herself to my side.

"I like your necklace," she says breathlessly, staring at the gold and diamond locket Daddy gave me right before his trial started. It has the word PRINCESS inscribed on the front of it because that's what Daddy calls me. When he gave it to me, he told me that no matter what happened, the locket would always remind me that I'm his Princess. Isn't that SO sweet? I never take it off, even when it doesn't go with what I'm wearing.

"Thank you," I say, smiling down at her. Finally, somebody who can speak more than one word (and give compliments, no less). Dakota is obviously an aberration from the rest of her family because not only does she display basic social etiquette, she's also cute. She's delicate and small-boned, with sandy blond pigtails and a smattering of freckles across her nose. I wonder if she was adopted.

"Did it cost a lot of money?" Dakota says in the next breath. "'Cause my mom says your dad used to be filthy rich until Satan caught up with him and punished him for—"

Sherri clamps her hand over Dakota's mouth, muffling the rest of her words. "Kids have such active imaginations, don't they?" she asks me over the top of Dakota's head, giving a little self-conscious laugh.

Yeah, right. I'm fairly certain Dakota didn't come up with that little scenario while she was conjuring up imaginary friends. Out loud, I merely reply breezily, "Oh, you know what they say—out of the mouths of babes."

Sherri smiles and lets go of Dakota's mouth. "Exactly." She looks around at Joe. "Don't you think we'd better get going, hon? I'm sure Caroline is just chompin' at the bit to see her new home."

Yep, that's me, chompin' at the bit. WTF? I think about taking advantage of the transition from airport to car to mention that my name is West, not Caroline, but then I decide to just let it wait. I'm tired, and there'll be time to bring it up later. Right now, I'm just looking forward to a long bath and a nap. Then, when I'm refreshed, I can assess the situation and decide what my next step should be in Project Return to L.A. With any luck, I'll be out of here so quick, it won't matter what they call me.

I spend the next three hours trapped inside a red minivan with a luggage rack, listening to country music while Sherri calls my attention to all the fascinating landmarks—"There's a brand-new Wal-Mart Super Center right there."

I'm actually grateful when I finally spot a wooden sign welcoming visitors and residents to Possum Grape, "Your Dream Hometown" (I'm not even going to comment on that last part). Per Sherri's instructions, Joe steers the minivan through the main part of the town so I can have a "tour." She obviously thinks seeing the town will make me excited, but instead it just makes me even more depressed. I mean, it's not that it's small—Beverly Hills is only six square miles—there's just nothing *here*. I see, like, a grocery store and a McDonald's. And a few gas stations.

How can people live in a place like this? I wonder as we pass a roadside stand offering GRANNY'S HOMEMADE BARBECUE.

There are no Starbucks, no boutiques, no restaurants. No wonder my mom moved to California when she was only seventeen.

"Our house isn't very far from here," Sherri tells me once I've seen everything. "We're almost there."

Thank God, I think silently. Except it turns out "almost there" doesn't mean the same thing in Arkansas as it does in California because twenty minutes later we're STILL driving. And although I'm not sure how it happened, we're somehow on a dirt road. I didn't even know the United States still *had* dirt roads. I thought they were all paved over when the pioneer people traded their covered wagons in for cars.

After five more minutes, we FINALLY turn into a gravel driveway with a rusty black mailbox marked REYNOLDS, Joe and Sherri's last name.

The first thing that pops into my mind when I see my new home is that Arielle lied to me. That whole positive visualization thing is a load of crap. Instead of Tara, Sherri and Joe's house looks more like . . . well, I don't even have a frame of reference for comparison. We don't have structures like the thing I'm looking at in Beverly Hills. So much for all my positive concentration on the plane. My Chloé dress was obviously a fluke.

"Well, what do you think?" Sherri says expectantly, as Joe maneuvers the minivan down the two, long ruts I assume are supposed to be a driveway and parks a few feet away from the crumbling front porch. Horror-stricken, I gaze up at the giant monstrosity looming over me. It's now official: I'm definitely in hell.

"It's, uh, very . . . peaceful," I stumble, unable to come up with anything better. I consider myself somewhat of an expert at spinning white lies (my dad works in Hollywood, after all), but Sherri and Joe's house is beyond even my capability for false flattery.

Fortunately, though, Sherri doesn't seem to notice. She nods vigorously, agreeing with me. "That's exactly why we bought this place. We just can't stand having neighbors right on top of us." She pats Joe on the shoulder. "Right, hon?"

Joe grunts, which I'm starting to think is his only method of communication, though I did see him give a macho wave to a couple of trucks we passed back on the main highway. Well, it wasn't a wave, actually. He just sort of lifted his index finger off the steering wheel for a couple of seconds.

"Of course, I'm sure it's nothing compared to what you're used to," Sherri adds. I glance at her sharply to see if she's being bitchy, but her expression is bland.

"What are you used to?" Dakota asks me, clearly fascinated. She sucks in a breath. "Did you live in a mansion?"

The question catches me off guard, and once again I falter for the appropriate response. I mean, now is probably not the best time to mention that I grew up in a ten-million-dollar home modeled after a famous castle in Italy. "It was just a house," I say lightly, hoping Dakota will cease and desist. Of course I have no such luck.

"But what kind of house?" she persists. "Was it like the mansion Annie lives in when she leaves the orphanage and goes to live with Daddy Warbucks? Did you have servants and a helicopter and—"

"Hush up," Joe orders Dakota sharply.

The van immediately falls silent. So he CAN talk! It's obviously a rare event, though, because even Clint looks up from the Game Boy he's been playing for the past three hours. I made a couple of futile attempts to engage him in small talk at the start of the trip, but he made it clear he wasn't interested in conversing with me, or basically even acknowledging that I'm alive.

Dakota shuts up even though it's obvious she's dying to ask me a few hundred thousand more questions.

Joe unbuckles his seat belt, which is apparently the signal that it's okay to get out of the van, because that's what everybody does.

I open my door and plop to the ground, making no effort to exit gracefully (it's an art, you know). I'm so grateful for the chance to finally stretch my legs and to escape further awkward conversation about my privileged background that I don't care about appearances. Plus, I doubt there's anybody around to notice whether or not I slide out sexily.

Stretching my arms above my head, I covertly survey the rest of my surroundings. I don't want Sherri to think I'm judging her or anything, even though I totally am. And if I were more like Simon and less like Paula, I'd be ripping this place to shreds right now.

I mean, it's a DUMP. The house seriously looks like it could collapse any moment. It's one of those giant farmhouses that was probably cute, like, seventy-five years ago, but now it's just falling down. The paint is peeling, half the shutters are missing, the roof is missing shingles—even the front door is askew. The only semi-attractive thing about the whole place is the pot of red begonias somebody put up on the porch railing. And there's no sign of a horse anywhere. So much for my notion of becoming an equestrian.

I lower my arms, trying to check out the assortment of shedlike structures on the property when a commotion to the side of the house catches my attention. I cut my eyes in the direction of the noise just in time to see what appears to be a pack of wild dogs round the corner, their long tongues lolling out of the sides of their mouths as they run. Directly. Toward. Me.

I fumble frantically for the door handle, but before I have time to dive back into the safety of the van, the biggest of the group—a giant black dog that is definitely not a member of the American Kennel Association—takes a running leap and knocks me flat on my back in the dirt.

The impact knocks the wind out of me, and I lie there for a moment, too dazed to move. Delighted with their new plaything, the dogs trample excitedly on top of me, eagerly sniffing my out-of-state smells. The black one licks me on the mouth.

Finally my lungs recover from the shock, giving me the ability to scream bloody murder. "Eeew! Get them off me!" I shriek, trying to protect my face.

Unfortunately, this only seems to make the creatures even more excited. They grab and lick at me furiously, like I'm some sort of new dog delicacy they can't get enough of. I think helplessly of the pepper spray in my purse, which, of course, is still in the van. And why the hell isn't anybody helping me? Is

THIS why Sherri wanted me here, so wild animals could rip me to shreds and devour my carcass?

Just as I'm about to see whether some of the moves I learned in my judo self-defense class are applicable to canines, a loud whistle pierces the air. The dogs perk their ears at the high-pitched noise. Then, as if by magic, they stop mauling me and trot back in the direction they came.

Wiping my face on my arm, I prop myself up feebly into a sitting position in the dirt. I should probably try to pull myself into the van in case they come back, but I think I'm in shock.

Joe is standing at the side of the house, squinting at the dogs. "Git on back to the barn," he orders them, pointing toward a dark red building about a quarter of a mile from the house.

Yes, get on back to the barn, I think, watching their wagging backsides as they trot obediently in the direction Joe pointed. Or better yet, why don't you guys just get on down to the highway and play on the yellow line?

Okay, just kidding—I didn't mean that. I would never condone harming an animal on purpose. I glance down at my outfit, which is covered in dirt. Unless, of course, said animal ruined my BRAND-NEW ZANE PORTER SUNDRESS! Damn it. And I was actually going to rewear this dress too.

Oh, well. I guess I should be grateful. They could have, like, ripped my face off instead of just shredding my outfit.

"Are you okay, hon?" Sherri asks, coming over to me.

Now she wants to know if I'm okay? Where was she thirty seconds ago when I was almost being killed?

I push myself to my feet. "I'm fine," I tell her, brushing off the skirt of my dress, which does nothing but smear the dirt in further.

She pats uselessly at the stain. "Sorry about that, hon. The dogs get real excited about visitors."

I can see Clint snickering over Sherri's shoulder. Jackass. I ignore him and give Sherri my best fake smile. "No problem." I will NOT lose my cool in front of these people.

"Why don't we go inside so you can change clothes?" Sherri says, giving me one last pat. "Then I can put some stain remover on this." She turns around. "Clinty! Will you carry Caroline's suitcases into the house, please?"

Clint scowls and walks toward the rear of the van. Ha. Serves him right. Too bad I'm not really going to live here. Then he'd have fifty suitcases to carry instead of the two miserly ones in the back of the van.

Dakota runs over and tugs on my arm. "C'mon," she squeals. "I wanna show you my room!"

I let her pull me into the house, amused. She IS really cute. I'll have to send her something adorable when I get back to L.A., maybe a cute charm bracelet or a necklace.

The inside of the house isn't any more impressive than the outside, though it's surprisingly clean. I don't get to check anything out too closely, though, because Dakota is practically running in her eagerness to show me her room. She leads me down a long hall and throws open a door covered in puppy and kitten stickers. "Ta-da!" she says proudly.

"Wow, this is beautiful," I tell her, stepping into the pale purple room. And it is, in a cluttered, unsophisticated sort of way. Sweet is probably the better word. Her furniture is white with little purple flowers stenciled around the edges, and a frilly white curtain hangs over the window. Toys sprout from every available surface, a hodgepodge of Barbies, stuffed animals, and plastic action figures. A bunk bed is pushed up against the wall in one corner, both bunks neatly made with matching purple Care Bear spreads.

"Which bunk do you want?" Dakota asks, excitedly dancing around in front of me. "I usually sleep in the top one, but Mama says I hafta let you pick 'cuz you're the guest."

"Excuse me?" I say blankly.

She does a little pirouette. "Which bunk do you want? The top or the bottom?"

I give a little laugh. Isn't she SO adorable? She wants me to sleep with her. That's crazy, of course, but maybe before I go back to L.A. we could have a little slumber party one night. I could paint her nails and put makeup on her and tell her about boys (the G-rated stuff, at least). It would be like I really was her big sister.

"I can't sleep in here," I tell her gently. "I have to sleep in my own room."

She stops twirling around. "But this *is* your room."

An uncomfortable feeling spreads through my lower stomach, but I keep the smile plastered on my face. "What do you mean, sweetie?"

"Me and you get to share a room 'cuz we're both girls. I was worried Clint would get you since y'all are the same age, but Mama says boys and girls can't share."

"But this is a big house," I protest. "There must be a guest bedroom I could stay in—not that I don't want to share with you," I add quickly when she gives me a hurt look. "But I'm sure you want your, um, privacy."

In truth, of course, it's *my* privacy I'm worried about. I mean, how am I supposed to plot my escape back to L.A. with a six-year-old watching my every move?

Her wounded expression disappears immediately. She slaps me playfully on the arm. "I don't need privacy, silly." She grabs my hand and pulls me over to the bed, apparently thinking the matter is settled. "So which do you want," she asks me again, "top or bottom?"

I stare helplessly at the extremely uncomfortable-looking beds in front of me. I know I said I was going to suck it up and handle this whole Arkansas situation with dignity, but this is too much. I can deal with wild dogs and riding in a minivan and Clint hating my guts, but I am NOT sharing a bunk bed with a six-year-old.

I open my mouth to tell Dakota jut that, but when I look down at her eager, upturned face, the words die on my lips. She looks so totally thrilled at the idea of us being roommates. I can't possibly crush her little bubble. Can I? I mean, I *can* be a real bitch sometimes, if the situation warrants.

Dakota grips my hand tighter and blinks up earnestly at me with her big blue eyes. Great. Now she looks even more adorable.

"Um, I guess I'll take the bottom," I say hoarsely. *For now*, I add silently to myself. I am so talking to Sherri about this as soon as I can corner her.

Dakota claps her hands together happily. "Perfect!"

I stare down at the bed, unable to believe what I have just agreed to, even if it's only for a couple of nights. A pink Care Bear smiles up at me from the spread, welcoming me to my new dreamland. "Yeah," I echo. "Perfect."

4

Hillbillies Are . . . Hot?

Things don't get much better after the bunk bed fiasco. In fact, they get worse, particularly when Sherri calls us all to the big wooden table in the kitchen for dinner.

My first official Southern meal consists of chicken-fried steak, mashed potatoes, some burnt-looking green things, and a basket of squishy white rolls. Nobody offers me a mint julep, but after the world's longest prayer, Sherri does place a glass of iced tea next to my flowered plate. At least I think it's iced tea. It's so sweet, it could just be sugar mixed with water. Wincing, I carefully spit the liquid back into the glass, hoping nobody is watching. I hate to be rude, but calories and carbs are precious commodities, and if I wanted to waste them I'd have dark chocolate or champagne, not tap water flavored with table sugar.

Setting the glass down on the table, I turn my attention

back to the mountain of food spread out in front of me, trying to keep my amazement from showing on my face. I've heard of people eating stuff like this, but I've never actually witnessed it in real life. Everyone in L.A. has either a personal chef or the Zone delivery system (I prefer Zone), neither of which would dream of serving anything REMOTELY like what's sitting before me.

Maybe I should buy Sherri a copy of the Zone Diet book, I think as I watch her pass the bowl of mashed potatoes around the table. It's got to be a matter of ignorance, right? Nobody would willingly put this stuff in their body if they knew better. Not that I'm a food purist or anything. I mean, I like a juicy hamburger from In-N-Out Burger as much as the next person, but that's an occasional kind of thing.

Sherri frowns as I hand the bowl to Dakota without putting anything on my plate. "Aren't you going to have any potatoes, hon?"

"Um, I don't really like potatoes," I tell her, which isn't really true. I like *baked* potatoes, dry and dusted with salt and pepper. Sherri's potatoes are thick as paste and probably contain my quota of fat and calories for an entire month.

"Have some extra okra, then. She smiles, dropping two giant spoonfuls of the burnt-green things on my plate.

Okra? WTH is okra? "Actually, would it be all right if I just had a salad?" I ask tentatively. "I can make it myself," I add quickly, not wanting to seem like a demanding guest. "If you'll just show me where you keep the ingredients."

Sherri gives me a tight smile. "I'm afraid we don't have

anything to make a salad with, hon. I already went over on the grocery budget to make sure we had something nice for your first night here."

Uh-oh. My request for salad has totally offended her. Time to backtrack and cover my ass, as Daddy would say. Which (as Daddy would also say) generally involves kissing some ass.

"That's okay," I say quickly, reaching for the platter of chicken-fried steak. I spear one of the golden brown patties with my fork. "I only asked for a salad because—er—I was afraid if I started eating any of this delicious food, I might I might not be able to stop. And, um, I might not leave any for the rest of you guys." Okay, that was, like, the lamest thing I've ever said in my life, but it seems to have worked. Sherri looks mollified. Pleased, even. Obviously complimenting her cooking was the right move.

"Don't you worry about that, hon," she says, glopping mashed potatoes onto my plate. "There's plenty more in the kitchen. We may not be rich, but we don't go without."

"That's—great," I murmur, trying not to look horrified as she piles my plate high with food. She doesn't really expect me to eat all this, does she? She's giving me, like, a Shaquille O'Neal–portion size. I look over at the others' plates to see how much food they have. Oh, God. Even Dakota has a Shaq-size serving. I *am* going to have to eat all this, especially now that I raved about my lack of self-control.

Gripping my knife and fork like weapons, I cut into the chicken-fried steak. I am so going to have to pay my trainer overtime when I get back to L.A.

When Dakota goes to take a bath after dinner, I close myself into my new Toys "R" Us bedroom and do three hundred ab crunches and two sets of push-ups. Then I call Delaney on my cell phone.

"I'm in hell," I say as soon as she answers.

"Oh no, is it bad?" She sounds shocked, as if it's inconceivable that being in a town called Possum Grape could be anything but fabulous. But that's Delaney for you, the eternal optimist. She's the only one of my friends who thought coming here would be "fun."

Of course, to be fair, Delaney is the only one of my friends who actually knows I'm *in* Possum Grape. Everyone else thinks I'm in Paris, visiting my dad's mother and her creepy poodle, François.

Shut up. I know I'm from a place where dressing your pet is de rigueur, but he wears a *smoking jacket*, okay? He's like a four-legged Hugh Hefner or something.

Anyway, I know it's cowardly to pretend like I'm in Paris, but I can't deal with all the crap everyone would give me if they knew what was really going on. I even made up this whole story about how nobody can call me because I'm taking this really strict French-immersion course that won't let me speak any English.

Hey, if you're going to lie, you might as well go all out. And I have enough on my mind without fielding phone calls from ten million people.

"It's worse than bad," I tell Delaney, trying to keep my

voice low in case there's anybody around to overhear. "It's hell. Their house is, like, falling down, the town is smaller than my backyard, I was just forced to ingest over ten thousand calories and God knows how many fat grams, AND I got attacked by wolves."

Delaney snorts. "Oh, come on. Wolves? Now you're just making stuff up to be dramatic."

"No, I'm not!" Wolves and dogs are practically the same thing, right? "I'm totally serious. They ruined my new Zane."

"Well, I'm sure they didn't *mean* to ruin your Zane," Delaney says soothingly.

I can't believe this. She's actually defending the Hounds from Hell. Clearly this conversation is going nowhere sympathy wise, so I change the subject. "Did Tristan call? Has he decided on the menu?" Tristan, to the uninitiated, is L.A.'s party planner extraordinaire. He's super hard to get, but he used to be friends with my mom "back in the day," as they say, so he always fits me in.

"He left a message on my phone, but I haven't called him back yet." She pauses. "Things have been kind of crazy today."

It's not exactly hard for me to figure out what—or rather who—is responsible for disrupting Delaney's day. I sigh. "What has Alice done now?" Alice is Delaney's mom, although she'd flip out if Delaney actually addressed her as "Mom," "Mother," or any other term that might indicate they were related. She's an L.A. shrink with a popular radio program, and she treats Delaney more like one of her patients than her daughter. Delaney actually used to call her Dr. McCann until

Delaney's dad put his foot down after Delaney started calling him Mr. McCann.

It's Delaney's turn to sigh. Alice is one of the few people who can puncture her perpetual bubble of optimism, which is insane considering Alice makes her living giving people advice on how to improve their relationships with others. "Just the usual," Delaney says wearily. "Bitching about me establishing my independence from you."

Oh, God. Here we go again. The whole "establishing her independence from me" thing has been going on since we were ten, when Alice discovered I was planning Delaney's outfits for school each week. She said Delaney was allowing me to "control" her and that she had to "construct her own identity." Which is total bullshit. The only person who's ever tried to control Delaney is Alice. I was just giving her fashion advice. I mean, yes, Delaney does sort of defer to my opinion on a lot of things, but that's because having an overbearing psycho mom like Alice has screwed up her head.

"Doesn't she have anything better to freak out about? I mean, she does know I'm, like, two thousand miles away, right?"

"Actually, she thinks you're on a completely different continent," Delaney corrects me. "We told her the Paris story too, remember? Apparently she considers you a threat from any distance."

"I'm flattered she's thinks I'm so powerful." Right. *I wish.* If I had even a fourth of the powers of persuasion Alice thinks I do, I wouldn't be in Possum Grape right now.

"There's also the fact that the show is on hiatus this month, which gives her extra time to focus on all my shortcomings," Delaney adds. "I seriously don't know how much longer I can stand it. This morning I almost told her to go you-know-what herself."

"Delaney, no!" I cry, alarmed. "You can't." Normally I'd be totally supportive of Delaney telling Alice off—even *pushing* her to do it—but the party is at Delaney's house and it would be EXACTLY like Alice to put the kibosh on it if Delaney ticks her off. "At least not until after the party," I add.

"Oh, please," Delaney says dismissively. "You know I don't have the guts to actually stand up to her. I just like to fantasize about it." She blows out a breath. "Let's not talk about it anymore, okay? It just upsets me."

"All right." I still feel a tad uneasy, but I know Delaney doesn't need me on her case too. "I think I figured out the reason Sherri brought me here," I say, changing the subject.

"Really? What is it?"

"Money."

"Money?" Delaney repeats blankly. "What does that have to do with your aunt wanting you to live there?"

"Everything," I tell her, which may seem like a totally random answer, but the more I think about the comment Sherri made at dinner, about them being poor but not going without, the more I'm convinced it's totally right. I mean, think about it: Obviously, they could use some extra cash, right? A LOT extra, judging from what I've seen so far. And what easier way to supplement their income than to house their rich, orphaned niece whose trust fund provides her guardian with a generous monthly stipend? It's all so simple, I'm actually embarrassed I didn't figure it out before.

"Think about it. She gets a monthly stipend for me living here—you know, to cover the cost of my room and board and stuff. What if that's the only reason she even wants custody of me? I could just write her a check and she could tell the judge she changed her mind."

"But wouldn't that be like she was blackmailing you? Forcing you to live there unless you give her money?"

"Who cares? If it gets me back to L.A., it's money well spent. Besides, it's not like I'd miss it or anything." In addition to passing on her thick hair and long legs, my mom also left me a big, fat trust fund.

"True," Delaney muses. "So when are you going to bring it up?"

I stare up at the bottom of Dakota's bunk, which is, like, five inches from my face. "As soon as humanly possible."

After Delaney and I hang up, I flop back on the Care Bears, intending to relax for a few minutes, but two seconds after I close my eyes, Dakota bursts into the room.

"I'm all clean and shiny!" she announces, spinning in a circle so that her pink Barbie nightgown flares out like a tutu.

I force myself to sound pleasant. "Yes, you are." I'm DEFI-NITELY talking to Sherri about the money thing as soon as possible.

She climbs onto the bed beside me. "Mama says it's your turn to take a shower now."

"My turn?" I echo. What, is the shower available by appointment only or something?

She picks up my cell phone and starts playing with it. "We have a schedule," she tells me, punching, like, all the buttons on my phone at the same time. "Mama put you after me."

Okay. So apparently you *do* have to have an appointment to use the shower. Yet another reason why I have to get out of here. For now, though, I guess I'll just have to deal with it since I can't exactly go without bathing. I slide off the bed. "I better go get all clean and shiny too, then, huh?"

"Will you read me a story when you come back?"

"Er—okay," I say, totally thrown off guard. Isn't she old enough to read to herself? "Why don't you pick one out and get in bed?" With any luck, she'll fall asleep before I'm done with my nighttime beauty ritual.

"Okay." She drops my phone and scrambles eagerly over to the bookshelf.

I grab the phone before she can punch any more numbers, then I get my overnight case and walk slowly down the hall toward the bathroom, which is on the other side of the house. Notice I said "the" bathroom. As in that's the only one they have, which I guess explains the shower schedule. Sherri says they're in the process of "fixin' things up," but I don't see anything that looks the least bit renovated. They're also in the process of saving money on electricity, which is why I practically need a Seeing Eye dog to get down the hall to the bathroom.

I've almost made it to the bathroom door when suddenly a male figure brushes past me and goes inside.

Clint, the jerk. "Hey!" I say loudly, outraged as the door shuts in my face. He KNEW I was going in there and purposely went in front of me. I lunge forward, intending to bang on the door, but somehow my feet get tangled up and I lose my balance. My makeup case goes flying out of my hand and lands on the wooden floor in front of me, bottles rolling out in all different directions. Damn it. I get to my knees and gather them up, even more annoyed. This is the second time I've found myself on the ground since I got here.

Standing up, I raise my fist to pound on the door, no longer concerned about being a sweet and charming houseguest. Besides, it's obvious sweet and charming aren't going to work on Clint. He's one of those people you have to treat like shit so that they'll respect you. Twisted, I know, but so are people, as Daddy would say.

To my surprise, when my hand makes contact, the door swings open a few inches. Clinty must have forgotten to lock it. Ha! Maybe I'll catch him doing something really embarrassing like masturbating. I push my way inside. "Don't you have any manners, you asshole—" My tirade cuts off abruptly, mainly because I've temporarily lost the ability to speak.

The guy leaning into the shower to turn on the water isn't Clint. What he *is*, however, is naked. And he's not just plain, old, birthday-suit naked—he's *hot* naked.

All thoughts of L.A. and Zane fly completely out of my mind. He turns away from the shower and faces me. "I'm s-sorry," I stammer, although I guess I don't look very apologetic considering I can't rip my eyes away from his extremely muscled body.

This is the part where either I should back out of the room or he should cover himself with the bath towel that's hanging on the rack in front of him, but neither of us moves.

"What's this about me not having any manners?" He crosses his arms over his chest and leans languidly against the counter, as if being nude in front of a strange girl is an everyday occurrence. Of course, with a body like that, it probably is.

"I thought you were Clint," I say stupidly.

His lips twitch. "I'm not Clint."

"No kidding." OMG, did I actually just say that out loud? What is wrong with me? Why am I acting like I've never seen a hot guy in the buff before? Perhaps because none of the guys I've seen had such dark eyes and bulging biceps and looked like some sort of Native American god? I'm not kidding; he looks like he came straight out of central casting. Daddy would flip.

He doesn't seem like he intends to offer any further information, so I ask the next obvious question. "So who are you, exactly?"

"Steven."

Again, no other information is forthcoming.

"Are you one of Clint's friends?"

"No."

OMG, talk about dragging information out of someone. "Are you related to Sherri and Joe?" *Say no*, I think silently. It would be tragic if a guy with such, um, assets, was off limits because of shared genetics. I mean, surely Sherri would have mentioned if they had another kid, but what if he's a nephew or a cousin or something?

"Do I look like I'm related to Sherri and Joe?"

Good point. "Well, do you live here or what?"

His teeth flash against the dark skin of his face. "Nah, I just come here to bathe." He slides the shower curtain back and steps inside, treating me to another look at his spectacular rear view before he pulls the curtain closed.

Alone on the fluffy bathroom rug, I go ahead and allow my jaw to drop, which up until now, I always thought was just a figure of speech. Wow. Maybe all that positive visualization on the plane worked after all. I know I was hoping for a curved staircase and horses, but what's on the other side of the shower curtain is WAY better.

I want to rip said curtain back and barrage him with more questions, but that might make me look interested. And everyone knows that under no situation whatsoever should you let a guy think you're interested. Especially a hot guy.

Pumping Dakota for information is a much better option. Forcing my mouth shut, I turn and head back to the bedroom to see what other interesting information can come out of the mouths of babes.

5
Pajamas and Pig Snouts

"D-O-R-O-T-H-Y, Dorothy the Dinosaur!"

At first I think the tune is part of a weird dream I'm having, but then the sleeping mask is suddenly lifted off my face and sunlight hits my unsuspecting eyes like a laser beam. I instinctively fling my arm over my eyes, wondering why on earth Maria opened the blinds before I've had a chance to put on my SPF. She knows how I feel about sun protection, even if I'm indoors. Those little amounts of UVA/UVB add up after a while, you know, and I am NOT getting crow's feet.

"Get up, sleepyhead," singsongs a high-pitched voice. A little girl's voice, not Maria's throaty, accented English. Memories from yesterday come back to me in a rush as my brain starts functioning.

Slowly, I peek over the top of my arm. Dakota is sitting

next to me on the bed, twirling my sleeping mask around by its elastic. Sitting up a fraction of an inch, I snatch the mask off her finger, jam it back on my head, and slide back down under the covers.

She immediately tries to remove it again, but I grab it before she can pull it all the way off. "Don't," I growl. I know I'm being mean, but I am seriously not a morning person. I don't reach optimal functioning level until about one in the afternoon. Last year I started a petition for my school to start at ten instead of eight, but the principal confiscated it, saying that the school schedule was not "up for debate." So much for living in a democracy. I mean, there are scientific studies that prove teenagers don't function well early in the morning. But do adults care? No.

Dakota jostles me. "Aren't you going to get up? It's already past six."

Six? In the morning? She's got to be kidding me. "Come back in four hours," I tell her, snuggling farther under the covers. I never get up before ten a.m. when I'm not in school.

"But you'll miss breakfast."

"I'm not hungry," I say, my voice muffled by the bedspread.

There's a brief silence. She's trying to think of some other way to persuade me to get up, I suppose. "Okay," she says finally. "But you're gonna get in trouble." The mattress shifts as she slides off the bed.

Thank God. Now I can go back to sleep. I'm just drifting off again when my sleeping mask is rudely ripped off my face for the second time.

"Hey!" I jerk up, ready to kill Dakota, but it's Sherri who's standing in front of me, holding my mask.

She looks annoyed. "Caroline, hon, get up. It's time to start the day." She lays my sleeping mask on Dakota's dresser.

She CAN'T be serious. "Er—I was kind of planning on starting my day a little later. I'm still pretty exhausted from yesterday. You know—jet lag and all."

"But if you sleep in, it will only make it harder for you to go to bed tonight. Then we'll never get you on a good schedule, will we?" she adds brightly.

I blink at her. Clearly her idea of a "good" schedule and mine are totally different. "I don't think it will matter. I'm pretty adaptable."

"It's time for breakfast," she says firmly. Apparently she doesn't give a flip about my adaptability. If Dakota weren't hovering in the doorway, this would be the perfect opportunity to bring up my whole check-writing proposition, but I figure it's not nice to discuss blackmail in front of a six-year-old.

"All right." Sucking in a deep breath, I force myself to push off the warm covers and slide out of the bunk bed.

Sherri's eyes widen to the size of dinner plates. "You're naked," she gasps.

"Huh?" I glance down at my lime green tank top and matching green-and-pink boy shorts, my standard sleeping attire. What is she talking about? I mean, I'm not dressed for a trip to Aspen or anything, but I'm hardly naked.

"No, I'm not," I say carefully, wondering if she's psychotic or something. "I'm wearing my pajamas."

"Pajamas?" she repeats incredulously. She shakes her head. "Pajamas cover your body. What you're wearing isn't covering anything." She closes her eyes and recites primly, "Proverbs 11:22 says a woman with no discretion is like a gold ring in a pig's snout."

"I'm, um, sorry?" I say, gaping at her. I'm totally not, of course, but I figure it's probably not a good idea to provoke a crazy person. Which she clearly is.

She opens her eyes and pats me awkwardly on the arm. "It's not your fault, hon. You can't help it—you haven't had anyone to give you any religious or moral guidance."

Before I can counter this incredibly offensive statement, she turns and disappears down the hall.

I remain rooted for almost a full minute, trying to digest the meaning of what just happened. Clearly, I need to hide all my Agent Provocateur bras and underwear as soon as possible, but beyond that, Sherri basically just told me she thinks my dad is a sucky parent, which is totally not true. He's not perfect, of course, but I also have Maria and she's practically a saint. Case in point: Do you know what Maria did after she put me on the plane to come here? She boarded another plane. Not to St. Barts or Jamaica or any of the other places my dad offered to send her while I'm gone, but to India. She's spending the next two months in Calcutta working at Mother Teresa's orphanage. How's that for freaking moral guidance?

Ticked, I stomp over to my suitcase. Ditching my immodest nightclothes, I pull on a pair of Juicy Couture sweats and a fitted white tank—my go-to choice for casual wear. Part of me would love to march out to breakfast in, like, a teeny-tiny bikini, but I'm not that stupid. Besides, I didn't bring a bikini.

Still, I'm not about to go around covered up from head to toe just because Sherri is a prude. Especially since I now know for certain that Mr. Hot Naked Guy and I are NOT related. Mr. Hot Naked Guy is how I've privately been referring to Steven—Mr. HNG for short.

C'mon, you didn't think I forgot about him, did you? No way. As soon as I left the bathroom, I came back and pumped Dakota for all the information I could get, even though I ended up having to read her THREE bedtime stories. Really, what am I, her nanny?

Anyway, this is what I found out in between *Tad the T-Rex*, *Emily's First Day of School*, and a super-condensed version of *Charlotte's Web*.

Mr. HNG does, in fact, live here. According to Dakota, he's lived here a "long time," which I suppose could mean anything from two days to ten years, considering that she's six. He's a foster kid, so I guess either his parents are dead or they're too crummy to take care of him. Which means he's even hotter than I originally thought. Guys from troubled backgrounds are sexy because of that whole "fixing" them thing.

Shoving my feet into a pair of flip-flops, I pull my hair back into a low pony and pop an Altoid before heading toward the kitchen. I feel gross, but hopefully I'll get a chance to groom more extensively after breakfast.

Dakota meets me in the hall where she's obviously been waiting for me. "You're up," she squeals. She bounces up and down, unable to contain her excitement. Is she a freak, or are all little kids this cheerful? I wonder.

Making a mental note to ask Sherri if Dakota is on Ritalin, I follow her to the kitchen. I couldn't care less about eating breakfast, but my body is in serious need of some caffeine.

Joe and Clint are already at the table. I take a deep breath and make my best effort to be pleasant. "Good morning," I say, sliding into the chair across from Clint. Joe makes a grunting noise from behind his newspaper. Clint scowls at me and looks away. Clearly, it's another glorious morning at the Reynolds' household. Seriously, though, what is Clint's problem, anyway? I mean, I get that Joe has that whole Neanderthal thing going on, but why does Clint act like he despises me? Did I offend him in another life or something?

Sherri is standing at the stove, stirring something in an oversize black skillet. She glances at me over her shoulder. "Caroline, hon, do you want bacon or sausage? Or both?"

I resist the urge to gag. Not only am I still mildly nauseated from last night's meal, but if I were stranded on a deserted island and had the choice of eating bacon and sausage or bugs, I'd choose the bugs.

"Neither, thanks. I'll just have some coffee." A LOT of coffee, I add silently.

"Coffee?" She smiles as if I'm a three-year-old who just said something amusing. "You're way too young to drink coffee, hon. It'll stunt your growth." She opens a plastic package and peels off several raw strips of disgusting bacon.

Um, is she serious? "I think that's just an old wives' tale." I strive to keep my voice light. "I've been drinking coffee since I was little, and I'm five nine."

Sherri isn't swayed. "But you don't know what sort of damage has been done internally, do you?" The frying pan sizzles as she begins dropping in strips of bacon. Clearly, she's oblivious to the irony here. I mean, she thinks coffee is unhealthy, but that eating dead animal flesh is fine?

"Besides, hon," she adds, dropping in the last piece, "we don't even have a coffeemaker."

No coffeemaker? Is she SERIOUS? That's like not having electricity or running water. Not that I expected them to have an espresso machine like the one Daddy bought me last year for Christmas, but I assumed they'd at least have a crappy Mr. Coffee.

"Want some of my chocolate milk?" Dakota offers, holding out her half-empty glass. Normally, the adorable milk mustache on her upper lip would make me smile, but without coffee, nothing is cute. Without coffee, life isn't worth living.

"No thanks," I say weakly. I slump in my chair, the beginning of a headache pulsing slowly behind my temples. Great, my body is already going into withdrawal. I'll probably get the shakes any moment.

"Me and Caroline are both named after states," Dakota announces to no one in particular. "North Dakota and South Dakota and North Carolina and South Carolina." She looks at me and smiles. "Right, Caroline?"

It's the perfect opportunity to correct everyone about my

name, so I do. "Actually, I'm named after West McCann, the character my mom was going to play in her first movie. That's what everyone calls me — West. Caroline is my middle name."

Clint looks up from his Game Boy. "*West?* That's stupid," he scowls. "It's not even a name. It's a direction."

OMG, there's a direction called "West"? I feel like exclaiming. Wow. I never knew.

"You mean like the Wicked Witch of the West?" Dakota asks.

I smile at her. She's as cute as Clint is awful. "No, just West."

Sherri brings the now-crispy bacon over to the table. "Clinty's right." She puts the platter in the center of the table and fists her hands on her hips. "West is a ridiculous-sounding name."

Right. As opposed to "Clinty," which is totally dignified. "A lot of people happen to like my name," I say defensively. "And so do I. It was special to my mother."

Sherri sighs. "Well, I guess it could have been worse, considering how fanciful your mother was. You could have just as easily ended up being 'Rainbow' or 'Sunshine.' Not that West is much better," she adds.

Clint snorts in agreement, prompting my foot to shoot out and connect with his shin under the table. Ooops. The caffeine withdrawal must be causing involuntary movements of my limbs. Because I'm WAY too mature to purposely kick someone because he and his mother are seriously ticking me off. That would be "unproductive," as Arielle would say.

"Ouch!" Clint scowls at me and leans down to rub his leg.

I draw my mouth up into a little "O" and put my hand over it in mock sheepishness. "I'm sorry. Did I bump you?"

He glares at me over the edge of the table, still rubbing his leg. "You didn't bump me, you kicked me," he says accusingly. "On purpose."

"Clinty!" Sherri scolds. "That's not nice. West said she was sorry."

I nod gravely. "Yeah, Clinty. I'm really sorry."

"See?" Sherri pats him on the back and goes back over to the stove.

I smirk at him across the table and feel a strange sense of satisfaction when he gives me a look capable of killing a small animal before turning back to his Game Boy.

If he's going to hate me, I'd at least like to feel as if I had something to do with it. Plus, Sherri called me West instead of Caroline. I think I'm making some real progress here.

Unfortunately, my quasi-good mood is short-lived because a few moments later Sherri plunks a heaping plate of food down in front of me. At least I assume it's food since the creamy brown stuff isn't anything I actually recognize.

"Biscuits and chocolate gravy," Sherri announces proudly. "In honor of your first official day here."

Dakota bounces eagerly in her chair. "Oooooh, can I have chocolate gravy too, Mama?"

Sherri shakes her head. "Not today, hon. This is West's special day."

"Oh." Dakota's shoulders slump.

"What, exactly, is chocolate gravy?" I ask, looking fearfully at the brown stuff.

Sherri laughs, obviously amused by my lack of sophistication. "Exactly what it sounds like, hon."

Which is EXACTLY what I was afraid she was going to say. *Man.* And I thought dinner last night was bad. What is with these people?

"Mama only makes it on special 'casions," Dakota adds, gazing longingly at my plate. I want to tell her to take it, please, but I guess that would probably tick Sherri off since she made it for my "special day." Even so, Dakota might as well take it because there's no way *I'm* eating it. I mean, I went along with the whole chicken-fried steak thing last night so I wouldn't hurt Sherri's feelings, but now things are getting serious. She's threatening my waistline here.

Except I still need to get on Sherri's good side so I can get out of this place. Damn. Maybe I can force down a few teeny-tiny bites and then push the rest of it around on my plate until this nightmarish breakfast is over.

I cut off a minuscule piece of biscuit with my fork and slowly bring the tiny morsel to my mouth. Taking a deep breath, I pop it inside. Other than a slight sweetness on my tongue, I can barely taste it, which hopefully means I'm not consuming very many calories. Okay. So far, so good. I'll just keep taking nonexistent bites until everybody is finished.

My plan works beautifully for the next fifteen seconds, but then Sherri sets ANOTHER plate in front of me. "Here's some bacon, hon. Those biscuits won't hold you until lunch."

What happens next is sort of embarrassing and MAJORLY gross, so I'll spare you the specifics. But just for the record,

I am NOT a puker. Really, I'm not. I watch plastic surgery on Discovery Health and everything. And when it comes to alcohol, I'm ALWAYS the hair-holder, never the heaver.

But when Sherri sets the plate of bacon next to me, my first thought is about reading to Dakota last night and the cute little pig from *Charlotte's Web*. And my next thought is about how, if I want to win this game of don't-tick-Sherri-off, I'm going to have to eat some of the bacon, too. Which would be like eating the cute pig from *Charlotte's Web*.

And the next thing I know, my insides mutiny, right in front of everyone.

Even though throwing up at breakfast has got to be somewhere near the top of the list of the Ten Most Undesirable Qualities in a Houseguest—right behind tossing lit matches at the draperies and cooking illegal substances in the bathtub— Sherri is surprisingly calm about the whole thing. In fact, she's *nice* about it, immediately hustling me to the couch to lie down and feeling my forehead for fever. Although I don't want to give her too much credit. I DID make it to the trash can beside the refrigerator, so it's not like she had to clean it up or anything.

"Are you sure you're okay?" she repeats, even though I've already told her that I'm fine.

"Yeah, I'm good," I say firmly, pushing myself into a sitting position. "It was just—ah—nerves, I guess." And the fact that you tried to make me eat a cute barnyard animal, I add silently.

She smiles maternally and clasps my hand. "There's nothing

to be nervous about, hon." She squeezes my hand. "And I want you to know that I understand exactly what's going through your mind right now, and I don't blame you one bit. I'd be thinking the same thing if I were you."

"Really?" I say, startled since what's currently going through my mind—besides that I really, really want to brush my teeth—is that she seriously needs to consider having her eyebrows professionally done. A higher arch and some brow pencil would make her look ten years younger, at least. Shut up—her face is, like, five inches from mine, okay?

"Of course. And it's totally normal. Nobody likes to feel like an outsider." She drops my hand and gets to her feet. "That's why I went ahead and wrote out some chores for you."

I'm abruptly jolted from my mental makeover of her eyebrows. Chores? WTH is she talking about?

"Joe thought I should give you a few days to get settled," she continues, reaching into the pocket of her jeans and withdrawing a folded-up piece of paper. "But I told him sometimes it's better to jump right in with both feet." She hands me the piece of paper.

With a sinking feeling in the pit of my stomach, I unfold it and quickly scan Sherri's handwritten list.

1. *Sweep front porch.*
2. *Trim weeds around mailbox.*
3. *Gather eggs.*

I reread number three to confirm that it really says "gather eggs." It does. Perfect! If I just had a kerchief and some talking mice, they could call me Cinderella instead of Caroline or West.

I glance up at Sherri. Obviously, this is some sort of joke. I mean, it's bad enough she's trying to force me to live here; surely she doesn't expect me to do manual labor as well.

She smiles and gestures to the paper. "I started you out with pretty easy stuff, but let me know if you have any problems."

I stare at her, horrified. OMG, this isn't a joke. She's totally serious. And not only that, but she thinks she's doing me a *favor*. I open my mouth to inform her that actually, I already have a very BIG problem, but her next statement causes the words to die on my lips.

"I know you're probably accustomed to being waited on," she adds, "but it'll be good for you to learn about the real world." Her voice sounds totally innocent, but I'm not an idiot. I can see the way she's trying to keep her mouth from curving up. She thinks this is funny! The spoiled Beverly Hills princess trotting around the farm in her Manolos and screwing everything up à la Paris Hilton and Nicole Richie on *The Simple Life*.

My limbs tingle as anger spreads through my body. The bitch! How dare she try to make me look like an idiot! I'm already here against my will; I REFUSE to provide these people with entertainment at my expense.

I set my jaw. My course of action is clear. Insane and totally driven by misdirected pride, but clear. Somebody tell one of the mice to fetch me a kerchief.

6

The Early Bird Catches the Rooster (and Maybe Rabies)

After I take a shower and brush—no, scrub—my teeth, I set out on my mission, which is basically to thwart Sherri's plan to make me look stupid. I'll show her; I'll do her chores like I was born wearing overalls with a hoe in my hand.

Armed with Sherri's instructions on the specifics of porch sweeping, weed trimming, and egg gathering, I go outside and get down to business. Number one on the list—sweeping the porch—sounds pretty straightforward, so I decide to start with that. Sweeping dirt into a dustpan, how hard is that? Actually, I don't even need a dustpan. It's a porch; I'll just sweep it right off into the yard. It'll take me, like, five minutes, and the actual physical part of sweeping will be good for my arms and shoulders. I could even throw in some lunges and turn the whole thing into a mini-workout. Jake, my trainer, is always saying how location and lack of equipment isn't an excuse for slacking off because you can always improvise, even if you're in the middle of nowhere. Of course, by "middle of nowhere," he meant, like, if your assistant screws up and books you a room in a hotel with a crappy gym. He wasn't talking about if a judge who hates rich kids sends you *literally* to the middle of nowhere, but I figure it's still good advice.

At least, it seems like good advice until I see a line of hideous brown spiders cruising along the porch like it's an arachnid expressway or something. Actually, though, it's not really the spiders that freak me out (arachnophobia is soooooo clichéd). No, what freak me out are the mutant wasps that suddenly swarm around my head. I say "mutant" because even though my knowledge of flying insects is limited, I'm pretty sure normal wasps are NOT the size of small birds. These wasps look like they escaped from a laboratory or spent their formative period frolicking in toxic waste or something.

Dropping the broom, I shield my face with my arms and run down the steps into the yard. Thankfully, none of the wasps follow. Apparently they're satisfied with merely having their porch back and don't feel the need to cause me extreme pain and swelling by attacking me with their freakishly long stingers.

The porch will have to wait, I decide, until I can come back with some bug spray, or maybe a small-caliber handgun.

I dig Sherri's list out of my pocket and reread number two. Trim weeds around mailbox. Lifting my head, I peer down the gravel driveway, looking for the mailbox, which is supposed to be at the end. I let out a disgusted snort. I can't even SEE the mailbox. The driveway must be, like, five miles long. If I wanted to continue the whole improvised-workout thing, I guess I could jog down there and get in some cardio. Except, thanks to the 200 percent humidity, I already feel like I'm breathing through a teeny-tiny straw. The mailbox weeds will have to wait too. Maybe later in the day the temperature will cool down to an icy ninety-five or so.

With the porch and mailbox put on hold, all that's left is the eggs. Panting, I pick up the frayed straw basket Sherri instructed me to the put the eggs in. The chicken house or coop or whatever you call it is only a few yards away from the house, so I decide to tackle that next. Maybe I can walk that far without having a heat stroke.

After making sure there's no sign of the Hounds from Hell, I walk toward the chicken house, feeling like Little Red Riding Hood with the stupid basket over my arm. The stench hits me before I'm even halfway there. I gag, barely able to keep myself from actually throwing up. The smell is putrid, worse than the smell inside this ghetto gas-station bathroom Delaney and I had to stop in one time when we got lost trying to go to a party in the Valley.

Somehow I manage to make it to the half-rotted wooden door. I push it open cautiously, wondering if there's a dead body or something in there. I mean, chickens don't smell like that, right? They're cute and fluffy and sit on cozy little nests. They smell . . . fresh, not like decomposing bodies.

Not so much, I realize when I finally get up the courage to

step through the door. Instead of fluffy, white hens happily sitting on nests of clean straw, these guys are scrawny, pitiful things slinking around a filthy enclosure that's not even a fourth of the size of my closet. I don't even see any nests. I glance around again, certain I must be mistaken. Where am I supposed to get eggs if there aren't any nests?

I pick my way to the other side of the enclosure, looking for some sign of a nest. The chickens move as far away from me as possible, clucking in disstress. Finally I spot a pile of dirty-looking eggs in the corner. I go over and gather them up, which takes all of two seconds since there are only four of them.

Mission accomplished, I straighten up and look admiringly at the ugly eggs nestled in the basket. *Ha, take that, Sherri*, I think smugly. The spoiled rich girl managed to gather your stupid eggs all by herself.

Feeling extremely self-satisfied, I turn to leave. And that's when it happens. I catch a fleeting glimpse of the wiry rooster before he does a kamikaze dive off his perch near the ceiling, but by then it's too late. He lands directly on my head.

Shrieking, I drop the basket and slap frantically at the insane bird. He clings determinedly to my scalp with his sharp talons, but I finally manage to land a felling blow. Screeching angrily, he drops to the ground, but instead of retreating like I was hoping, he whirls around and flies at me again. I lash out with my foot, knocking him away, but once again, I'm too late. A burning sensation spreads through my index finger. The feathered bastard bit me.

Unfazed by the not-so-lethal kick from my flip-flop, the rooster charges forward again. This time, however, I'm prepared. I do what any poised young woman who is trying to prove she can survive farm life would do: I tear out of the chicken house screaming bloody murder.

To my credit, though, I only scream for a few seconds. Then I hyperventilate.

I stay bent at the waist, sucking in shallow breaths until finally someone comes to my side to help. Well, he comes to my side, at least.

"What the hell is wrong with you?" Even in the middle of respiratory disstress, I have no trouble recognizing the voice of Mr. HNG. Dragging my head up from between my knees, I straighten up shakily to look at him.

Which does nothing to help my already erratic pulse. He's wearing more clothes than last night, but not much more, just jeans, work boots, and a baseball cap turned around backward. His chest is still bare. And bronzed. And muscled. And he has some sort of manly looking tool (a wrench, maybe?) in his hand, resting it on his shoulder.

"A rooster bit me," I tell him.

He looks me up and down. "Where?"

Squeezing my eyes shut so I can't see the blood, I hold out my hand.

I feel his big hand encircle my wrist, but he releases it after just a few seconds. "That's just a scratch," he says derisively.

My eyes fly open. "What?" I yank my hand away from him and bring it to my face, fully expecting to see a big gash and lots of blood, but he's right. It's just a scratch. I feel strangely dissappointed. Not that I wanted to have a major injury or anything, but if you have to go through the trauma of being attacked by a rooster, shouldn't you at least have something to show for it? Suddenly another, more awful thought occurs to me.

"Oh, God. What if it had rabies or something?" That pen was filthy, after all. "Maybe I need to go to the hospital."

He gives me the same amused grin from last night. "It'll be all right." With that comforting reassurance, he saunters away toward a shady area where a car is up on blocks with its hood open, which I guess explains the wrench. Wow. None of the guys I know can do anything more to a car than turn the key in the ignition.

"How do you know that?" I call after him.

"This is the South. If you start foaming at the mouth, somebody'll shoot you."

I spend the next hour on my cell, making Delaney Google roosters and their potential disseases. In keeping with their StoneAge existence, Sherri and family don't have the Internet, not even a crappy dial-up connection. I haven't even seen a computer, come to think of it. They probably use a typewriter. Or a quill feather dipped in ink. Or maybe a stone tablet.

"So you're sure it doesn't say anything about rabies?" I ask Delaney for the third time.

"*Yes!* I'm sure, okay? It doesn't say anything about rabies."

Delaney is annoyed with me, but I don't care. Traumatized people need lots of reassurance. "What about bird flu?"

"You don't have bird flu," Delaney growls. "We already went over that, too."

Once I'm finally convinced I'm not going to die, I realize I have to ask Sherri point-blank about the money thing. I intended to broach the matter subtly at an opportune moment, but this is no longer just a matter of getting back to my life in L.A.; it's a health issue. I mean, I may have narrowly missed contracting rabies or bird flu today (please, God), but who knows what might happen tomorrow? I could be bitten by a rattlesnake or eaten by a coyote or something.

"So how much money do you need?" I ask matter-of-factly after I've finished explaining that I know what the deal is. We're standing in the cramped laundry room together, folding towels. Okay, technically, *Sherri* is folding towels. I'm just sort of making them into lumpy squares.

Sherri is silent for a moment then she says slowly, "You think I want custody of you because we need money."

A pang of sympathy shoots through me. It must be totally embarrassing to admit that you took in your niece because you're broke. I put my hand on her shoulder to show her there are no hard feelings. "It's okay. I understand why you did it. I'm sure I'd do the same thing if I was poor."

She throws down the towel in her hand and whips around to face me. "Well, isn't this just a fine howdy-do," she says hotly, fisting her hands on her hips.

I put a hand on my throat, startled. I'm not exactly sure

what a fine howdy-do is, but I can tell from the way sparks are shooting out of her eyes that it's probably not good.

"I've spent the past fifteen years trying to bring you here with your family," she continues, "and your second day here you accuse me of being a thief!"

"I'm not saying you're a thief. I just—" I break off as the first part of her statement finally registers. I frown at her. "What do you mean you've been trying to bring me here for the past fifteen years? I didn't even know you existed until you showed up on our doorstep this summer." Okay, so I *sort of* knew she existed. You know, because of the Hanes Her Way and all. But I'm trying to make a point here.

Actually, while we're on the topic, you've probably been wondering exactly *why* I never had anything to do with Sherri, considering she's my mom's only surviving relative and all. And the answer is . . . I don't really know. It just never came up. I mean, L.A. is a LONG way from Arkansas, you know? And, actually, Sherri isn't my mom's full-blooded sister. They have different fathers.

"Didn't know I existed! How can you say that?" Sherri exclaims incredulously. "I know I wasn't able to contact you in person," she continues, her voice becoming apologetic, "but what about my letters?"

"Your letters?" I repeat, my confusion growing by the millisecond. "What letters? I've never gotten anything from you but some ugly underwear at Christmas." I pause. Okay. That didn't come out exactly the way I intended. Great. Now she'll probably go off about howdy-dos again.

I wait for the tirade, but instead she blurts, "Well, I'll be a monkey's uncle."

Hmmmn. A monkey's uncle. I wonder if that's better or worse than a howdy-do? Since I have no idea, I do the safe thing and keep my mouth shut.

"I should have known," she continues, talking more to herself than me. "But I honestly never thought Jean-Claude would stoop that low."

"What are you talking about?" I ask, startled at the mention of my father. "Stoop that low about what?"

She finally looks at me. "I knew he hated me, of course, but I never dreamed he'd purposely keep my letters from you."

I hold up my hand. "Whoa, wait a minute. Are you trying to say the reason I never got any of these letters you supposedly wrote is because *my father stole them*?"

"Well, that's obviously what happened, isn't it?" she says simply.

I can't help it; I laugh. The idea of my handsome, powerful father sneaking outside to the mailbox every day so he can intercept my mail is so ridiculous, it's funny. My father doesn't even handle his OWN mail, for heaven's sake. Hello, that's why God invented personal assistants.

I shake my head, still laughing. "No offense, Aunt Sherri, but I find it hard to believe that my father has been filching my personal correspondence." I refrain from adding that the more plausible scenario is that she's LYING. She's probably never sent me so much as a postcard.

Sherri shrugs, undeterred. "Maybe it was that Spanish woman, then."

"Maria?" I say incredulously. My amusement rapidly dwindles. I can handle Sherri accusing my dad of being underhanded, but now she's moving into dangerous territory. Over the years, I've had a handful of people make the mistake of thinking they could diss Maria because she's "hired help," and it never fails to royally piss me off.

Not to mention that Maria is the LEAST likely person to take something that doesn't belong to her. I mean, the woman won't even let me get her a free gift basket when I'm at an event. And we're not talking about a couple of bottles of crappy body lotion and a scented candle. It's serious swag she's passing up.

"Look, let's just forget about the letter thing, okay? It doesn't matter. I want to know what you meant when you said you'd been trying to bring me here for fifteen years."

She huffs out a breath. "Hon, I didn't go to L.A. on a whim, or because we need money. I've been trying to get custody of you since the day the Good Lord took your mama in that plane crash. Four times I've gone to California. And if it wasn't for your father, you'd already know that." She shakes her head. "I always told Crystal that man was lower than a snake's belly in a wagon rut."

"But that doesn't make sense," I protest, ignoring the fact that she just referred to my father as—whatever the hell she just said. "How could—"

She cuts me off. "Wait here," she says curtly. "I've got proof, if you don't believe me." Before I can say respond, she steps around me and out of the room.

If I had anywhere to go besides Dakota's bedroom, I would

totally leave, but as it is, I just lean obediently against the dryer. The only way this could get any weirder would be if Sherri came back with, like, an actual monkey.

After a minute or so, Sherri returns with a manila folder. She thrusts it into my hands. "Here. Read."

I open it curiously. I can't imagine what she wants me to read, but whatever it is, I'm sure it's fascinating. And yes, I'm being sarcastic. Except when I start to read, I realize it actually IS fascinating. Or maybe the word I'm looking for is "disturbing."

I flip through the stack of papers, barely able to believe what I'm seeing. The folder is full of court documents or, more specifically, petitions for custody of "minor West Caroline Deschanel." Filed by Sherri Reynolds.

I look up at Sherri, dumbfounded.

"See?" she says happily. "I told you I was telling the truth."

7

My Mother Was an Alien, and Other Family Secrets

"Your mama always had a premonition she wasn't going to live to be an old woman," Sherri tells me, taking a sip of lemonade. We've left the cramped quarters of the laundry room in favor of the "sunroom," which is how Sherri refers to the screened-in porch at the back of the house. It's sweltering in the sunroom, but the screens are torn in several places, so at least the mosquitoes have a nice, shaded area in which to suck our blood.

"Nobody ever paid her any mind, of course," she continues. "We just thought she was being morbid. Crystal was always dramatic like that, you see."

I hold my glass of lemonade, barely listening, even though she's talking about my mother. I'm still trying to come up with a plausible reason for why my dad never told me about Sherri trying to get custody of me. I mean, doesn't that seem like something I should have known? If he wasn't in a medium-security prison two thousand miles away, I would SO confront him right now. Except he'd probably just say something annoying like he was trying to protect me.

I force my attention back to Sherri, who is still reminiscing about my mom. "I promised Crystal the day you were born that I'd take care of you if anything ever happened to her, but with your daddy's money and his big-shot lawyers, I never had a chance. Not that I didn't try," she adds quickly. "You can see from the papers in that folder that I tried."

"But why would my mother want *you* to take care of me instead of my dad?"

"Crystal didn't want you to be raised in a place like California, even when she was alive," Sherri continues, not answering my question. "She had it all worked out. She thought if she modeled for two more years, she'd have enough money to live on for the rest of her life. She was going to come back here and build a house."

This makes even less sense. "But what about my dad? He wouldn't have wanted to live here."

She gives me a sympathetic look. "I don't think he was ever a factor in the equation, hon."

"But they were madly in love! It was in *People* magazine!"

"Sometimes the press exaggerates."

"No, they don't! I mean, they weren't exaggerating about that." Okay, I know every little kid wants their parents to be totally in love. I saw *Parent Trap* when I was little, like everybody else. And I know most parents AREN'T totally in love. But mine were different! They were! Daddy has told me tons of stories about him and my mom.

"I'm not saying she didn't love your father," Sherri says evenly. "But she wanted what was best for you, and she knew that didn't include the kind of lifestyle Jean-Claude lived."

"What do you mean 'the kind of lifestyle' he lived?" I retort. "From what I've read, she was living that lifestyle too." I have no idea why Sherri's doing this. I mean, I accept that she tried to get custody of me or whatever, but why is she making up all this stuff about my mom and dad? Acting like my mom was going to divorce him and move back to Arkansas?

"Crystal never wanted you to be raised in California," she repeats. "She wanted you to be brought up in a good, Christian environment, not a heathen place like Los Angeles." She takes a deep breath. "Lord knows what kind of damage that place and your father have done to you, but don't worry—now that you're where you belong, I'll never let you go."

"You don't understand. I *have* to speak with him."

"Inmates aren't permitted to receive phone calls, miss," the operator repeats in her flat, lifeless voice.

"But this is an emergency," I plead. "It's a matter of life and death." Which is totally true because my dad is alive and my mother is dead. And I'm totally pissed at both of them.

The operator sighs heavily as I start to sob quietly into the phone. "Hold the line," she says wearily. "I'll see if there's anything I can do."

There's a mechanical click, and then elevator music fills my ear. I immediately resume normal breathing, relieved I didn't have to resort to full-blown hysterics to get her to help me. I already knew that *residents* ("inmates" sounds so gauche) aren't supposed to get phone calls, of course, but I don't care. I HAVE to talk to my dad and I can't wait until the third Sunday of the month, or the first full moon, or whenever the hell it is he's allowed to make a phone call.

Because after spending the afternoon listening to Sherri, I now realize that I'm in SERIOUS trouble. The situation here is much, much worse than I originally thought. Not only does Sherri think she's fulfilling some sort of sacred duty to my dead mother, apparently she also thinks she's been entrusted with the responsibility of saving my immortal soul. I mean, how do you argue with someone who is convinced she's on a mission from God? Why couldn't she have just been after my money like a normal human being?

I brood over my incredibly bad luck until finally the music is interrupted by my dad's panicked voice. "Princess? What's wrong? Are you okay?" For an instant I'm so touched by his obvious distress that I almost forget I'm mad. *Almost.* "Why didn't you tell me Sherri has been trying to get custody of me since I was a baby?" I demand, skipping the pleasantries. No doubt this will be a short call and there's a LOT I want to say.

"What?" He sounds confused. "Is there—"

I cut him off. "Sherri just showed me a folder full of all the custody petitions she's filed over the past fifteen years. For custody of *me*."

"And?" He sounds unimpressed.

"And?" I repeat shrilly. "All you can say is 'and,' like it's no big deal? Why didn't you ever tell me?"

"What purpose would telling you have served?" he replies reasonably. "Except to upset you?"

"For one thing, maybe if I already knew I had a crazy aunt who was trying to kidnap me, I wouldn't have been so stunned when she showed up on our doorstep this summer," I shoot back. "Maybe if we'd been better prepared, the judge wouldn't have awarded her custody."

"We were prepared," he responds sharply. "Luke handled Sherri the last time she popped up, when you were about ten or so. He knew she'd show up again when she found out about my conviction."

"*Luke* knew about this?" I say incredulously, remembering the way Luke had feigned shock when I called to tell him about Sherri showing up at the house. "And he never said anything? I thought attorneys were required to tell their clients stuff that could affect their lives."

He chuckles softly, amused by my naïveté. "You're not his client, sweetie. I am." Translation: He's the one signing Luke's checks, not me.

By now I've gone from angry to furious, so I don't care if what I say next is hurtful. "Sherri said Mom was going to quit modeling and move back here to raise me. That she wasn't going to stay married to you."

"That sounds like something Sherri would say," he says, totally unruffled.

His complete calmness is disconcerting. I can understand—and indeed expected—him to be blasé about the custody thing, but I figured he'd go ballistic when he found out about Sherri's claim that my mom was planning to divorce him. "So it's not true?" I say uncertainly.

"I'm sure Sherri *thinks* it's true," he replies. "But as we both know, sometimes a person assumes a thing is true when, in fact, it couldn't be farther from reality."

"So it's not true," I repeat, annoyed by this nebulous response. I need straightforward answers right now, not him tap-dancing around the point.

He must sense that I'm close to losing it, because suddenly his tone becomes more understanding. "Let me try to explain something about Sherri, Princess. Even though she and your mother were very close when they were little, Sherri never approved of your mother going into modeling. Their parents had raised them in a very strict, religious environment, and to Sherri, the idea of a woman making money off her looks was immoral." He laughs, remembering. "'Prostitution for pictures' is what she called it. And, of course, she despised me," he adds wryly. "I wasn't your mom's agent, I was her pimp."

Although this new info about Sherri is certainly enlightening, it still doesn't answer the question of whether or not my mother was really hatching some secret plot to leave my father and raise me in Arkansas. "So you're saying Sherri made up all that stuff about Mom quitting modeling and moving back to Arkansas?"

"Crystal made it very clear to Sherri that she had no

intention of giving up her career, or moving away from L.A., and I think that hurt Sherri very badly. She felt like Crystal was abandoning her. When Crystal died, I think it was just easier for Sherri to convince herself that all those things had been true. And somewhere along the way she decided it was her duty to rescue you from me, the vile, immoral man who, as she saw it, killed her sister," he finishes wryly.

"Gee, and I was worried you were going to tell me something serious."

"I know you're upset, Princess, but I'm going to fix this. I promise. You'll be back home with Maria soon."

"How soon?" I ask immediately.

"As soon as I can."

"Well, when will that be, exactly?" I shoot back, not caring if I sound like a spoiled brat. "Because my party is in two weeks."

"I thought we agreed you and Delaney were going to postpone the party," he says tersely.

"No, you *asked* us if we would postpone it," I clarify. "We never said we would." And if he had any conception of how much effort it took to coordinate my fashion show, he'd realize why postponing it is such an unreasonable request. Do you have any idea how hard it is to accommodate the schedules of thirteen professional models, four hair and makeup people, an in-demand deejay, AND Tristan? The answer is—practically impossible. Short of the apocalypse or Prince William asking me to elope with him that weekend, there's no way I'd reschedule this thing.

"Okay. So now I'm *telling* you to postpone it." To a stranger, he'd probably sound calm, but I recognize the hint of temper in his voice. Daddy isn't accustomed to people disregarding his requests, especially me.

The line is quiet as he waits for my response, but I don't say anything. I don't have to. The silence says it all. We both know he can't tell me to do anything. He's not even my legal guardian anymore.

The operator's voice cuts through the unspoken tension. "Miss, your time is up. I have to disconnect you now." The abrupt reminder of my dad's current location makes me feel instantly guilty. *You're not the only one in a less-than-ideal situation, West.* I chide myself. And at least I still have my freedom. Relatively speaking.

"Bye, Daddy," I say hastily. "I love you."

"I love you too, Princess."

The operator cuts us off immediately, so it could have just been my imagination, but it almost sounded like his voice broke.

8

Wal-Mart Couture

I'd like to say the next morning is better, but that would be lying. Like yesterday, Dakota wakes me up at the ungodly hour of six in the morning. This time, though, I don't even bother to protest. I just stumble out of bed and follow her into the kitchen like a zombie, still wearing the yoga pants and T-shirt I wore to bed. After yesterday's pig snout lecture, I'm not taking any chances.

I steel myself for whatever disgusting food Sherri tries to serve me this time, but to my surprise I find a banana and a plate of toast waiting at my spot. "I thought it might be easier on your stomach," Sherri explains, gesturing to the food.

Even though I have now officially declared her my enemy, I'm oddly touched by this gesture of thoughtfulness. But then I remind myself that it's as much for her benefit as mine since I highly doubt she wants a repeat of yesterday's breakfast either.

Unlike yesterday, I make no effort to speak to Clint or Joe, and they reciprocate the gesture. Once again, Steven is nowhere to be seen. I nibble on a piece of toast and try to look attentive as Dakota tells me all about her favorite cartoon character who is a cucumber or an eggplant or something. She's like the Energizer Bunny on speed. Seriously. And she's NOT on anything; I asked. Not even Ritalin. Apparently all this energy is au naturel, which leads one to wonder if maybe she *should* be on something.

When everyone is finished, I wait for Sherri to whip out her list of chores and tell me I have to milk a cow or shear a sheep or something, but instead she claps her hands together and says cheerily, "Okay, everybody, go get dressed. We're going to buy your school clothes."

Dakota immediately looks excited. "Can I get tennis shoes like Molly's?" she asks eagerly. "With charms on the laces?"

"We'll see," Sherri answers.

"I'm going to the feed store," Joe mumbles, pushing back his chair. He puts his dirty plate in the sink and slips out the back door, clearly eager to escape.

I get up too. "You guys have fun," I say, trying to conceal my glee. As soon as they're gone, I'm SO going back to bed. "I'll see you when you get back." Taking a cue from Joe, I pick up my dirty plate and walk over to the sink.

"What do you mean, hon?" Sherri asks. "You're going with us."

I whirl around, startled. "Me? Why would I go?"

Sherri laughs. "Well, you're still in school, aren't you?"

"Yes, but what does—" I break off as I realize what she's getting at. OMG. She's talking about me going to school *here*. In Possum Grape.

What am I supposed to do now? I think, panicked. I never even considered the possibility of having to go to school here. I just assumed I'd be out of here before it was an issue. Of course, that was before I knew Sherri thought she was on some sort of mission from God.

Finally, I say hoarsely, "It's okay. I don't need anything. I have plenty of clothes."

"I thought a teenage girl could never have enough clothes," Sherri says teasingly. She gets up from her chair. "Y'all go get ready," she orders, making a shooing motion with her hands. "I want to get to Wal-Mart before the crowd."

Dakota shoots out of her chair like a rocket, the possibility of new shoes hyping her up even more than normal. *So much for going back to bed*, I think glumly, trudging after her. Instead, I get to go to Wal-Mart.

By the time I reach the bedroom, Dakota has ditched her nightgown and is struggling to pull a pink T-shirt dress over her head.

I move toward her. "Here, let me help you." I grasp the material with both hands and tug it down over her head.

"Thanks," she says breathlessly when her head finally emerges through the opening. "I thought I was going to be stuck in there forever."

The serious expression on her face makes me laugh. "No problem." As I'm moving toward my suitcase to get my own clothes, Dakota blurts, "Will you fix my hair?"

The question catches me totally off guard, just like when she asked me about the bedtime story.

"Like yours?" she adds.

"Mine?" I echo, even more startled because my hair looks like total crap. It hasn't been touched since I pulled it into low pigtails after washing it last night.

She nods. "I want to look just like you. You're prettier than Barbie."

Twenty minutes later, Dakota and I climb into the minivan with our hair parted on the side and secured in identical low pigtails. Hello—how do you say no to someone who tells you you're prettier than Barbie? I even topped my frayed jean skirt with a pink tee to match Dakota's dress.

"Don't y'all look cute!" Sherri exclaims, beaming at us from the driver's seat. Clint is beside her in the passenger seat playing (what else?) his Game Boy.

"West fixed my hair," Dakota says happily.

"She did a good job," Sherri assures her, putting the van in gear.

"You look like a dork," Clint says, not glancing up from his Game Boy.

Yeah. Like *he* has room to talk.

"Wanna color?" Dakota holds out a glossy coloring book with a bright purple pony on the cover. "You can pick your page first." She blinks at me with those freaking giant blue eyes, but this time I'm actually able to resist her, mainly because I'm already half asleep even though we've only been driving for, like, three seconds.

"I need to rest for a few minutes," I tell her, already leaning my head against the door. *I seriously have to talk to Sherri about this bunk bed situation*, I think groggily. I'm not getting anywhere close to the eight hours of sleep necessary for proper skin rejuvenation.

By the time we get to Wal-Mart, I have a lovely imprint of the window on my cheek and something that looks suspiciously like drool on my arm. Which is gross, but let me tell you—it's nowhere *near* as disgusting as what Sherri wants me to try on once we're inside the store.

Now, before anybody gets defensive and accuses me of being a snob, you have to understand something: Clothes are my LIFE. They're my inspiration, the way I express myself, my reason for living. I'm a connoisseur of clothes, just like some people are connoisseurs of wine. And it just so happens I was born into the kind of lifestyle that allows me to indulge my passion to the fullest.

So, while there's nothing wrong with buying mass-produced clothes at low prices—some of the stuff is actually even cute—it's just not something I *do*. Or want to do. I mean, if that's all you can afford, that's one thing, but I can buy whatever I want.

"This would be perfect for church," Sherri says, holding up a flowered dress that *would* be perfect for church on, say, a ninety-year-old woman. As the newest member of the family, Sherri decided we should shop for me first. She thrusts the dress at me.

I take it reluctantly and drape it over my arm on top of the two other hideous outfits she's picked out. "Uh, I thought we were shopping for school clothes."

"Well, you can wear it to school, too, hon," Sherri answers, moving on to the next row of rounders. I glance over at Clint, who is leaning against a concrete post, still playing his Game Boy. I'm starting to understand why he always looks so dorky.

I toy with the idea of telling Sherri that Buddhists don't go to church, but that would probably just further convince her she needs to save my soul.

Dakota tugs on Sherri's shirt. "Mama, when are we going to my section? We've been in this part forever." It's the first time I've seen Dakota act whiny, but instead of being annoyed, I silently urge her to keep on. In fact, it would be great if she could bust out in full-on temper tantrum. Maybe throw herself on the ground and beat the linoleum with her fists. Anything to divert Sherri's attention away from making me into Clint's female counterpart.

"Don't act selfish," Sherri chastises Dakota, frowning down at her. "Remember, Jesus is watching you."

The warning has its desired effect. Dakota releases Sherri's shirt and glances around fearfully, as if expecting Jesus to step out from behind a rack of wind pants and reprimand her.

Wow. Maria would be impressed. She used to try that sort of stuff with me, but it never worked. I mean, once I figured out there were, like, a gajillion kids in the world and that Jesus—or, more typical with Maria, the Virgin Mary— couldn't possibly keep tabs on all of them, it didn't seem like much of a threat. Now, Santa Claus, on the other hand, he worried me. Because, you know, he had all those elves he could use for spies.

Sherri works her way through the racks until I'm loaded down with clothes. "Now, go try those on," she directs, motioning toward the dressing room. "I can't afford to buy it all, so we'll just narrow it down to the stuff we really like."

We don't like anything, I retort silently. *We* don't need to try anything on. *We* don't want to be here.

"Now can we go to my section?" Dakota begs. She's either forgotten about Jesus watching her or has decided to take her chances. "Please? While West is trying on?"

I wait for Sherri to say something like, "Satan kidnaps little girls who are pushy about their school clothes," but she surprises me by giving in. "All right. We'll walk over there," she concedes. "But first we have to get Clinty some underwear."

Eeeew. I guess I should be grateful about being forced into the dressing room if shopping for Clint's underwear is my other option.

"I'll check on you in a little bit, hon," Sherri tells me, taking Dakota by the hand. She glances around for Clint. He hasn't budged from his spot against the post. "Clinty!" she yells across the twenty feet of space separating them. "Come on, we're going to get your underwear!"

I walk toward the women's dressing room, shaking my head. Poor Clint. You almost have to forgive him for being so ill-tempered all the time. If Sherri were my mother, I'd probably be in a permanent bad mood too.

The entrance to the women's dressing room is blocked by a shopping cart filled with plastic hangers. A bored-looking woman in a blue smock is standing beside it, sorting the hangers into piles.

I wait for her to acknowledge me, but she just continues robotically reaching into the basket. Finally, I speak up. "May I use a dressing room?"

"How many," she says in a bored tone, not even glancing at me.

"Um, I guess just one," I reply uncertainly. Are Wal-Mart dressing rooms really small or something? "Or do you think I need two rooms?" I thrust out my pile of clothes to get her opinion.

Now she actually looks at me. "I'm not asking how many rooms you want," she says slowly, as if I'm an idiot. "I'm asking how many things you're trying on." She jerks her chin toward a sign behind her. "You can only take in three at a time."

I peer around her at the sign. Sure enough, it asks customers to "Please limit articles in dressing room to three items."

I look back at hanger-woman. "Why can't you take in more than three things?" Not that I care, since I don't even want to take in one thing, but now I'm curious. I mean, that seems like a pretty arbitrary rule.

She shrugs. "It keeps the dressing rooms from getting too messy. And it helps cut down on shoplifting."

And this is EXACTLY why I don't buy low-end clothing. Call me crazy, but I prefer to shop in places that don't automatically assume I'm a criminal. And, like, why would I *want* to steal this stuff, anyway?

The woman moves away from the shopping cart and plucks something off the counter. "Here," she says, handing me a plastic tag. "Take in three things and leave the rest on the counter. After you finish with the first three, you can switch out."

I take the tag from her unenthusiastically. Damn. I was hoping she might decide I looked like a shoplifter and ban me altogether. With a sigh, I pluck three things off my arm—including the horrible flowered dress—and dump the rest on the counter. Satisfied, hanger-woman moves the shopping cart and directs me to the first room on the right.

Even *I'm* tired of my bitching, so I won't even comment on the dressing room. It doesn't matter, anyway, since this isn't like real shopping. In fact, what am I even doing in here? I think suddenly. Sherri is across the store; she won't know whether I actually try anything on or not. I'll just stay in here for a few minutes and then leave. I can use the time to call Delaney.

I dig my cell out of my purse, but as I start to dial, my eye falls on the flowered bedspread—I mean, dress. And it suddenly occurs to me that it would be REALLY funny if I put it on and sent Delaney a picture with my cell phone.

Chuckling at the thought of Delaney's expression when she sees my "church" dress, I strip off my clothes and pull the thing over my head. After I zip the back, I survey myself in the mirror. I look like I'm wearing, well, a bedspread. Delaney is going to pee her pants.

I grab my cell phone to capture this lovely vision of myself, but a second later I realize the lighting in the dressing room is too poor to get a very clear image. I'll have to go outside the dressing area, where it's brighter.

Aware that Sherri could return any second, I hurry out of the room. Hanger-woman is still by her shopping cart. She flicks a glance at me as I squeeze around her, but doesn't comment on my outfit. I guess Wal-Mart doesn't pay on commission.

I go over to the three-way mirror directly across from the fitting area to see if I look as hideous from the back as I do from the front. Holding my arms out to the side, I peer over my shoulder.

"Very sexy," comments a deep voice.

Startled, I drop my arms and whirl around. Steven is behind me. The corner of his mouth tugs up as he surveys my outfit. "You going for a new look?"

I blink, unable to believe that he's actually standing there. I mean, this is getting ridiculous. Could I not ever run into him at, like, a semi-normal moment? Just once? "Yeah, what do you think?" I ask teasingly. I hold out the skirt and pretend to model. I refuse to act embarrassed, even if he does look totally hot and I look like a dork.

"Like I said, very sexy. Are you getting the matching orthopedic shoes?"

"Probably. At least if Sherri has anything to do with it." I let go of the skirt. "So what are you doing here?" I ask him, my expression sobering. "Is Sherri determined to buy you horrible clothes too?"

He shakes his head. "Nah. I just wanted to see if you survived."

For a few seconds I have no idea what he means, but then I realize he's talking about yesterday with the rooster. "Oh, that. Yeah, nobody had to shoot me."

"Good thing. I might have felt guilty for not taking you more seriously." He glances around. "Where's the rest of the fam?"

"Buying underwear for Clint."

"Gee, sorry I'm missing that."

"So, what's your deal, anyway? How come you're never—"

"Steven!" Sherri appears out of nowhere, interrupting the million-dollar question of why he's never around. "You remembered the shopping trip," she says proudly.

I slant him a look. Ha! He *is* here to shop. I hope Sherri puts something hideous on him, too. Except I'm not sure he's capable of looking hideous, even in Wal-Mart clothes.

Sherri turns from Steven to me. "West, that dress looks gorgeous on you." Her smile is so wide her face is in danger of cracking in half. "We'll have to get you some shoes to go with it."

Steven's smile is as wide as Sherri's. "I told her the exact same thing."

9

Close Encounters of the Pot-Fueled Kind

"Does your head feel better yet?" Dakota calls down to me from the top bunk.

I glance up from the new biography of Coco Chanel I'm reading just in time to see her do an awkward toe touch as she plummets from the top bunk to the floor. She lands with a thud.

I sigh. It's the twenty-second time she's done that particular move in the past hour. I know because I've been counting. Not that I *want* to count, but it's kind of hard to concentrate on Coco when Dakota is conducting a mini-Olympics above my head.

"Don't you think that's kind of dangerous?" I ask her as she picks herself up off the carpet and starts climbing the wooden ladder again. "You're going to break a leg or something."

"My bones are really strong," she informs me.

Fine, I think silently. I did my duty as the semi-adult in the room. She's not my kid, so it's not like I can yell at her or anything.

She hangs her head off the side of the bunk and looks down at me. "So, do you feel better? Can you go?"

I lay the book beside me and do my best to look like I'm in pain. "I don't think so. My head hurts really bad."

In case I had any doubts about Sherri's commitment to saving my soul, this morning she announced that she's enrolled me in something called Vacation Bible School, which is apparently some sort of class where you study the Bible. I mean, come on—*Vacation* Bible School? That's an oxymoron if I've ever heard one. Studying the Bible hardly qualifies as a vacation. I should know; Maria made me go to a Catholic elementary school.

Anyway, I was DYING to go, but darn if I didn't come down with a migraine early this afternoon. A really, really horrible one. You know—the kind that only goes away if everyone leaves you alone and lets you sleep for twenty-four to forty-eight hours.

Of course, I'm totally faking. I've never had a migraine in my life. Luckily, one of Daddy's girlfriends used to have them all the time, so I pretty much know the deal. And since I'm exercising my acting skills, I also told Sherri that I can't do any more "chores" because I have really bad allergies and that the pollen count is too high. Am I a genius, or what?

I feel guilty about pretending to be sick to get out of going to church (okay, not so much), but them being gone will provide me with a prime opportunity to prowl the house and do a little snooping. If I can't bribe Sherri into sending me back to L.A. with cold, hard cash, maybe I can uncover some deep, dark secret I can use for real blackmail.

"They have cookies," Dakota says hopefully, as if the lure of sweets might convince me to go anyway.

I struggle to keep myself from snapping at her. I never realized how persistent little kids are. "Maybe you can bring me one back."

She shakes her head. "Miss Annie only lets us take one each."

"Dakota! It's time to go!" Sherri's voice resonates down the hall.

Dakota's upside-down head disappears as she shouts, "Coming, Mommy!" A second later her body plummets to the floor for what I hope is the last time. Picking herself up, she smoothes her cotton dress and slips her feet into a pair of battered white sandals before rushing out the door. "Bye, West," she calls breathlessly over her shoulder.

A few minutes later I hear the minivan's tires crunch on the gravel driveway. Breathing a sigh of relief, I sit up in bed and try to call Delaney. I swear when her voice mail picks up yet AGAIN. It's like the tenth time I've called her, and I'm starting to get seriously worried. Delaney always answers when I call, even if she's in the middle of something important like a massage. She's never MIA like this.

After leaving yet another message, I get out of bed, slide into my comfy Chanel ballet flats, and slip out of the room to start my search. I decide to start with Sherri and Joe's bedroom first, since that's the most obvious place where I might find some dirt. Maybe I'll get lucky and Joe will have a stash of kiddie porn (eeeew) under the bed or something.

Yeah, right. I can't even imagine Joe having a normal sexual thought, much less a deviant one. I wonder if he and Sherri even have sex now that they've satisfied that whole "go forth and procreate" thing by having Clint and Dakota.

Trying to banish all images of Sherri and Joe's sexual relationship from my mind, I set off toward their room, which is on the other side of the house, near the bathroom. I'm almost there when I suddenly hear strains of rock music. It's not very loud, but I know it wasn't playing a few seconds ago, which means I'm not alone in the house like I'd thought. I freeze, fear snaking up my spine. OMG, what if I'm in here with some sort of intruder? One who listens to old Ozzy Ozbourne as he steals people's valuables and rapes and murders their unsuspecting houseguests?

Okay, put like that, it DOES sound a little crazy, but who else could it be? Even as the question pops into my mind, so does the answer: Mr. HNG.

I strain my ears as the music crescendos. It sounds like it's coming from upstairs, but I thought the second floor was basically condemned until they renovated, which is clearly scheduled for sometime never. Puzzled, I walk to the foot of the stairs and peer up into the darkness. Yep. There's no doubt about it; the music is definitely coming from somewhere up there. I glance down at the stairs, which are basically just misshapen pieces of plywood nailed together. Ugh. They look pretty precarious, but the curiosity factor is too great to resist.

I place one foot on the bottom step and press tentatively, testing it out. It seems okay. I ease the rest of my weight onto it slowly. So far, so good. I do the same thing with each step until I'm all the way at the top.

I'm standing in the middle of a bunch of exposed lumber and plastic tarps, but a partially cracked door to my left has both light and Ozzy spilling out of it, along with the unmistakable scent of marijuana.

When I push it open, a shiver passes over my skin and it's not because it's cold. Although you'd think it would be hard to top seeing him bare-ass naked in the bathroom and half naked doing manual labor, this sighting of Mr. HNG is even more awe-inspiring.

He's in bed, propped up against some pillows, languidly smoking a joint. A white sheet is draped low across his hips, and of course he's not wearing a shirt.

If he's surprised to see me suddenly standing in his doorway, he doesn't show it. "Do you ever knock?" he asks lazily, taking a drag.

"No." I push the door open all the way and step inside. "Not lately, anyway."

I check out his room, which takes all of, like, three seconds. Other than his naked chest, there's not much to see. A chest of drawers in the corner, a wooden chair, some free weights — that's pretty much it. It's impossible to deduce anything personal about him from his lair, except that he's probably not gay. No self-respecting gay guy would live in a room this inadequately decorated, foster home or not.

Steven watches me from the bed. He holds the joint out. "Want some?"

I stare hesitantly at the proffered gift. Normally I don't do any sort of substance, unless you count the occasional drink at parties, because the few times I have done anything, it felt a little too good, if you know what I mean. And an extended stint in rehab would totally screw with my career plans, so I figure—to borrow a phrase from the eighties—it's better to "just say no."

On the other hand, I have had a hellacious past few days. Who could blame me for indulging in a bit of a chemical escape? "Sure." I walk over and pluck the joint out of his hand. "Scoot over," I order, plopping down on the bed. Surprise flickers in his eyes, but he obediently shifts over. It's no wonder he's shocked I'm capable of normal behavior, I guess, considering our previous encounters.

I settle myself against the pillow. "So, what's the deal with this Casper thing you've got going on?" I ask, taking a deep drag.

"My Casper thing," he repeats, looking amused.

I pass the joint back to him. "Yeah, you know—how supposedly you live here, but no one ever sees you? You just materialize for a few seconds, and then poof"—I make a magician-esque gesture with my fingers—"disappear. You're like Casper the Friendly Ghost."

"What makes you think I'm a friendly ghost?"

I give him a look. "You know what I mean. So what gives?" I ask impatiently when he doesn't respond. "Why doesn't

Sherri make you get up at the crack of dawn and gather eggs? Because if you have some sort of secret weapon you use against her, I'd like to borrow it."

"Farm life not agreeing with you?" He laughs, passing the joint back to me.

"Uh, that would be putting it mildly."

"And what terrible misfortune has brought you to the Reynolds' Home for Wayward Teens?" he asks, pulling the joint out of my lips before I've even finished inhaling. He's obviously trying to avoid answering my questions, but for the moment, I let it slide.

"Well, if you want the *Reader's Digest* condensed version, my mom's dead, my dad just went to prison, and it turns out Sherri is my long-lost aunt."

Another person would probably find the part about my mom and dad the most startling, but the first words out of Steven's mouth are "Sherri is your aunt?"

"Unfortunately." I reach over and yank the joint out of HIS mouth.

He's so amazed by my revelation, he doesn't even notice. "Man, that blows," he says, shaking his head.

"Tell me about it," I say wryly. "And to make matters worse, she apparently thinks that because of my 'upbringing,' I'm on a one-way street to hell unless she can manage to save my soul."

"Man," he repeats, still shaking his head. "And I thought I had it bad."

"All right," I say, thrusting the joint toward him. "I told you my story, so come on—out with it. What misfortune brought you here?"

He shrugs uncomfortably as he plucks it out of my hand. "Kind of the same thing as you, I guess. Except both of my parents are in prison. Oh, and Sherri's not my long-lost aunt," he adds dryly.

"Wow. How did *both* of your parents end up in prison?" I ask, fascinated. "Did they rob a bank Bonnie and Clyde–style or something?"

He smiles sardonically. "No, you have to have more than two functioning brain cells to rob a bank. They were convicted for operating a meth lab."

I try not to act shocked, even though I am. People on meth are usually SERIOUSLY messed up. "Oh. So, um, do you think they really did it?"

"Let's see . . . ," he says sarcastically. "Since they ran it out of our house, yeah, I'm pretty sure they did it."

Okay, I guess I walked into that one. Somebody seriously needs to do a book on the proper etiquette when discussing people's incarcerated relatives. Martha Stewart, maybe, since she has personal experience with the whole prison thing.

We smoke the rest of the joint in silence. By the time I hand it back to him for the last time, I'm feeling MUCH better about the past few days and basically life in general. I lean back against the pillow. "They should so make pot legal."

"No arguments here." He tosses the roach into an ashtray on the table beside the bed and turns back to me. "So," he says huskily, draping his arm around my shoulder, "tell me what you want to do now"—his gaze flicks down to my necklace—"Princess." The suggestiveness in his voice is blatant, but it's not like I can accuse him of being forward or anything since I'm the one who barged into his room and crawled into bed with him. "Actually, my name's West," I say lightly.

He brushes my cheek with his hand. "I like Princess better," he says softly, an instant before his lips close over mine.

Even though I've only technically had half a joint, I blame the pot for what happens next, which is that we basically start ripping each other's clothes off. Except he's only wearing jeans, so the amount of ripping I have to do is considerably less.

Okay, I know you're probably thinking I'm a total slut, but I swear I'm not. I NEVER do this. But he's just so . . . *irresistible.* Plus, like I said—the pot is clouding my thinking.

It's only when he murmurs, "Wait a sec and I'll get something," that I come back to my senses.

"I can't do this," I say abruptly, pushing him away. I sit up and start fumbling through the covers for my discarded clothes. I locate my shorts and shirt almost immediately and put them on, but my bra is nowhere to be found. I jerk frantically at the covers.

"Looking for this?"

I glance up. Steven is holding out his arm, my bra dangling from one of his fingers. He looks amused.

I yank it out of his grasp and stuff it in my pocket. "I'm leaving."

"So I noticed."

"I'm sorry," I say awkwardly.

"No need to be sorry." He folds his arms behind his head and shuts his eyes. "It's a free country, Princess."

My heart is still slamming against my chest when I reach Dakota's room. By now you're probably really wondering WTH is up with me, so let me try to clarify some things.

First off, let's get the Big Dirty Secret out of the way: I'm a virgin. Yes, that's right—a VIRGIN. As in I haven't had sexual intercourse. With anyone. Ever. I've come close a few times, but no cigar. Or penis, as the case may be.

And before you ask—no, I'm not a virgin because I have some sort of Jessica Simpson religious hang-up about being a virgin on my wedding night (not to be smug, but look how well that turned out). And no, I'm not a prude or frigid or socially inept or any of the other stigmas the V-word seems to carry.

The reason I haven't had sex is simple: I haven't wanted to. You see, I want my first time to be with somebody special, somebody I feel a connection to, somebody I respect and who respects me. More specifically, I want my first time to be with Zane.

Except Zane doesn't respect me yet—but that will all change once he sees my fashion show at the party. Right now he only knows me as a rich socialite, but after he finds out I'm a designer and sees my work, he'll realize I'm so much more than that. And then I'll lose my virginity to him. Which is why I had to stop things with Steven just now, even though it was REALLY hard (no pun intended). I knew I would have regretted it because he's not the right person.

There. Clear as mud? Good.

10

Go, Possums!

Possum Grape High School has exactly one thing in common with my school in Beverly Hills: They each have the word "school" in their names.

My school in L.A. is in a brand-new, twenty-thousand-square-foot complex complete with a sparkling Olympic-size swimming pool, a state-of-the-art computer lab, and an espresso bar. Possum Grape High is in a run-down building from the seventies complete with a musty gym, a computer lab partially made up of electric typewriters, and an auditorium partly submerged in water. And I'll give you three guesses as to what the school mascot is. Here's a hint: It has a long tail, and plays dead. . . .

I'm not kidding about the auditorium—when the student body files into the dimly lit space for the back-to-school announcements, the first thing I notice is that the first five rows of seats are under two feet of water, at least. And the really strange thing is that everybody acts like this is totally normal.

"Um, is there some sort of plumbing problem?" I ask the girl shuffling in behind me. She gives me a weird look, like she has no idea what I'm talking about. I gesture toward the front. "You know, because of all the water?"

"Oh, that." She shrugs. "It always does that after it rains."

"Why doesn't somebody fix it?" I ask, but the girl has already disappeared into the crowd. I consider asking somebody else, but I seem to be the only person the least bit concerned that the room is half flooded. The other kids pay as much attention to the water as the paint on the walls, probably because they're all too busy staring at me.

And it's not the good, wow-she's-hot kind of staring either. It's more like the wow-she's-a-freak sort of staring. I guess I do look sort of out of place in my spike heels, True Religion jeans, and red Betsey Johnson top. I mean, there are some other girls who are dressed somewhat similarly, but they're all in mall clothes, the kind of stuff Delaney and I wouldn't be caught dead in. And, unlike me, none of them appear to have spent forty-five minutes with a double-barrel curling iron coaxing their hair into perfect, tousled waves.

I pick a seat at the back of the auditorium, both to avoid the water and to prevent people from gawking at me without at least being forced to turn their heads. As I'm settling my Louis V in my lap, I catch sight of Clint drifting in with the rest of the crowd. He's with what looks like his clone, another guy with the same buzzed-off hair and dork clothing.

As if he can sense my thoughts, Clint turns his head and looks right at me. Crap. I hate it when I get caught staring. But I also hate it when people who get caught staring look away really quick to try to pretend like they *weren't* staring, so I hold Clint's gaze and give a little wave to him and his twin.

He scowls and immediately darts into the row of seats closest to him, sitting down so that his back is to me.

I smile to myself. He really hates me, poor guy.

A paunchy man with a receding hairline walks onto the stage and taps the microphone. He introduces himself as Mr. Bullard, the principal, and launches into a long list of announcements, which I immediately tune out. Normally I'm pretty attentive to stuff like that, but it's not like I'm going to be at this school long enough to need to know any of his boring information, so instead of paying attention, I occupy myself with searching the auditorium for Steven. I feel like I owe him some sort of an apology for the other day. Even though he didn't exactly seem hurt or anything, it's still not cool to just run out on somebody like that.

I'm still scanning when the room suddenly erupts into a loud clatter of noise as people start getting up from their seats and gathering their stuff. I guess the announcements are over and I didn't hear one word. Oops. I realize I don't even know where I'm supposed to go for my first class. I keep seeing people referring to these white, index-type cards that I assume are class schedules, but I don't have a clue where they got them.

Oh, well. Maybe I can just hang out in the bathroom or somewhere all day. I could sketch or, even better, sleep. The combination of Dakota's bunk bed and my forced caffeine withdrawal is really starting to get to me. I think jealously of Delaney, who is probably at this very moment drinking a triple-venti latte. Actually, she's still asleep at this very moment since it's, like, two hours earlier in L.A., but when she wakes up she'll drink a triple-venti latte. OMG, I would KILL for a triple-venti latte right now.

I follow the tide of the crowd out of the auditorium. I suppose I should go to the office and try to sort out the whole where-I'm-supposed-to-be thing, but instead I go into the girls' bathroom just outside the auditorium.

Ugh. The scent of industrial air freshener assaults my nostrils. Gross. At my school, the bathrooms smell like real lilacs. I walk to the last sink and plop my Louis V down on the ledge under the mirror. My hair is fabulous, if I do say so myself. Too bad it's totally wasted on this bunch. How was I supposed to know girls around here take the whole concept of "wash and wear" literally? I briefly consider brushing out the waves and pulling it back into a ponytail just to be a little less conspicuous, but purposely destroying an awesome hairdo just seems so . . . wrong. Like a crime against nature or something.

Instead, I take out my makeup case and start touching up my eye makeup. Normally my makeup is infallible, but the humidity here is kicking even MAC's ass.

I'm sweeping Satin Taupe across my brow bone when a cute blonde with short, curly hair bursts through the door. She drops her backpack on the floor and starts pulling paper towels out of the dispenser. I observe her covertly through the mirror as she wets the towels and starts rubbing vigorously at a stain on the hem of her top, which is surprisingly cute. It actually looks like a Versace I had last season. I watch her for a few seconds, debating whether I should intervene, but finally I can't stand it anymore. "Here," I say, pulling a disposable stain-remover cloth out of my bag. I walk over to her and hold out the little paper package. "Try this."

"Oh, thank you," she says gratefully, dropping the useless paper towels in the sink. She rips the package open and dabs at the spot with the little cloth. As if by magic, the stain disappears.

She throws her arms around me, almost knocking me down. "Thank you so much! I thought it was ruined for sure."

"Er, you're welcome," I tell her, taken aback by her reaction. I mean, it's not like I did the Heimlich maneuver or anything. It's just a stain-remover cloth. I always carry them for emergencies exactly like this.

She lets go of me, still chattering. "Seriously, I was going to be so ticked if it was ruined. It took me, like, three days, just to cut the fabric."

"You made it?" I ask, immediately interested.

She nods. "Yeah. I make a lot of my clothes."

"Really?" I wasn't planning on making any friends since I'm not going to be here long enough to bother, but now I'm totally intrigued by this girl. "Did you design it too?"

She shakes her head. "No, it's from a pattern—Vogue. My mom owns the fabric store here in town, so I get a discount."

"Vogue has some good patterns," I murmur, taking a step back to survey the top from a distance.

"Do you sew?" she asks quizzically.

I nod absently, still examining the top. "Yeah, since I was little."

"Wow, you totally don't seem like the kind of girl who would know how to sew."

I glance up, amused by her obvious shock.

A pink flush is spreading up her cheeks. She has one of those round, angelic-looking faces with the cute button nose and rosebud lips. "I mean, not many people sew anymore," she says quickly. "Especially girls our age."

I smile so she'll know I'm not offended. It *is* shocking that a girl like me sews, but when you want to be a fashion designer, it's kind of a handy thing to know. "That's so true. It's like a lost art or something."

"Exactly." She looks relieved. "That's what my mom says too. She says when I'm an adult I'll have a skill that not many other people will have. So, you should totally come down to the store sometime. It's not that big, but we have some cool fabric. I'm Sophie, by the way," she finishes breathlessly, tucking a blond curl behind her ear.

"I'm West. West Deschanel."

"I know," she blurts. "You're Clint Reynolds's cousin. Everybody's been talking about you." This time, her cheeks turn scarlet.

"It's okay." I laugh, amused by her hyper-concern for my feelings. "I understand."

"It's just that we hardly ever get new students," she explains. "Everybody's known one another since kindergarten.

Small towns, you know? And it's not that they're saying anything bad about you. It's just that you're kind of like . . . I don't know—an exotic animal or something."

"So you're saying people think I look like an elephant," I deadpan.

Sophie looks horrified. "Nothing like that! It's just that—"

"I'm kidding," I cut in. "Look, I totally understand if people are talking about me. It doesn't bother me. I grew up in a place where gossiping is practically a professional sport." My last two words are interrupted by the shrill, metallic sound of a bell.

"Shit!" Sophie yanks her backpack off the floor and slings it over her shoulder. "That's the tardy bell."

I choke back a giggle. It's funny to hear her say a curse word, I guess because she's got that whole blond-cherub thing going on.

"Listen, do you want to hook up at lunch?" she says hurriedly. "I could introduce you to some of my friends."

"Er—" I hesitate for a second, not sure how to answer. Like I said, I wasn't planning on making any friends here, but Sophie seems really nice, plus she's looking at me with that same big-eyed stare Dakota has. "Sure, that'd be great."

"Cool," she says, backing toward the door. "I'll meet you outside the entrance to the cafeteria."

Considering I have no class to go to, I guess I don't have to worry about being tardy, so I stay in the bathroom after she's gone, finishing my eye makeup. After it's perfect again and everything is back in my makeup bag, I glance impatiently around the bathroom, tapping my foot. I can't decide what to do. My original plan of staying in here and sketching is a no-go because of the yucky air freshener (I have extremely sensitive olfactory nerves), but I certainly have no interest in actually attending class. I'll just have to find a different place to hide out, I finally decide, picking up my purse.

The thought of checking to make sure the coast is clear before I open the door never occurs to me (hey, I'm not used to skulking around school, okay?), and when I push it open—to my absolute horror—it connects with a body.

"Shit!" the unlucky person and I say in unison.

When I peer around the door, I almost don't even recognize the person on the other side. But, of course, I'm not used to seeing him with clothes on.

"You trying to kill me or something, Princess?" Steven asks, rubbing his forehead.

I stare at him, dismayed. Great. Way to apologize, West. Smack the guy unconscious. "Oh, my God. I am SO sorry," I say earnestly. "Are you okay?"

He bends over, still rubbing his head. "I don't know. I feel kind of dizzy."

Panicked, I rush forward and grab his shoulders to steady him. OMG, what if I fractured his skull, or gave him a concussion or something? I didn't push the door that hard, but what if it hit him at just the right angle? You know—like how a pencil can kill you in a car crash if you're going a certain speed?

"What can I do?" I say urgently. "Do you want me to get someone?"

He shakes his head. Suddenly, he straightens up and grabs me around the waist, pulling me to his chest. "Why don't you just kiss it and make it better?" he asks, flashing me the same mischievous smile from yesterday.

"You jerk!" I start, struggling to get out of his grip. "I thought you were really hurt." I glare at him accusingly, but his attention is focused on something behind me.

"Busted," he says under his breath.

"Why aren't you two in class?" booms a male, distinctively authority-figure-type voice over my shoulder. Crap. I turn around and look into the face of the pudgy principal from the auditorium. Double crap.

Steven's voice is mockingly earnest. "She's a new student, sir. She needs help finding her class."

"I'll take it from here, Mr. Kinney," the principal snaps. "You go find wherever you're supposed to be."

"Yes, sir!" Steven gives him a little salute, then mutters, "Have fun."

"Fuck you," I mouth silently.

"Anytime," he mouths back.

"Come along, young lady," the principal says gruffly, taking my arm. "Let's get this sorted out."

Thanks to Steven, I'm forced to suffer through biology, English, history, and Spanish II—or, more accurately, Spanish for two-year-olds, since that's the fluency level of both the class and the teacher. Not that I'm bilingual or anything, but I WAS raised by a native speaker, so I'm a bit more proficient than

"Mi nombre es West,*"* which is the sentence we work on for the entire period. Unfortunately, when I ask the teacher if I can switch to French, she just laughs and tells me it isn't the French who are trying to take over the country.

By the time the bell finally rings for lunch, I'm exhausted from the sheer effort of (A) staying awake; (B) ignoring all the people staring at me; and (C) pretending I'm not totally in lust with Steven.

Sophie is waiting for me outside the cafeteria. "Here she is!" she squeals excitedly to the three girls standing with her. She rushes forward and hugs me. What is her deal with all this touchy-feely stuff?

She turns to the stranger-girls, still holding my arm. "This is West," she says proudly, presenting me to them like I'm a brand-new puppy or something. Two of the girls greet me warmly, but the third one just frowns and mumbles something unintelligible.

The girls enter the cafeteria, and Sophie leads me along behind them, clutching my arm in a mother hen-ish sort of way. Normally I'm the one leading Delaney around protectively, so this is a real role reversal for me, but I follow Sophie meekly, allowing her to guide me to a table.

I can feel people's eyes on us, staring. A cacophony of whistles and catcalls assaults us as we pass a table of beefy-looking guys I assume are football players or some other type of jocks. I was mistaken when I said PG High has nothing in common with my school in L.A. It does have one thing that's the same: guys. Ogling you, that is.

Except in L.A., the guys who ogle you are often hot. Here in PG, they are not so hot, with the exception of Steven.

Okay, to be perfectly fair, a couple of the football players we just passed might rank hottie status, but it's easier to lump them all together as NITLs (Not in This Lifetime).

The girls come to a halt in front of some empty chairs at a partially full table in the middle of the cafeteria, not far from the jocks. For a moment I worry that Sophie is going to keep holding my arm, but thankfully she lets go and pulls out a chair. I collapse into the chair next to her and watch disinterestedly as the four girls open identical brown lunch sacks. I have one too, thanks to Sherri, but I'm not the least bit hungry, mostly because I can imagine only too well what's inside the sack.

"Aren't you eating?" Sophie asks, her brow wrinkling with concern.

I shake my head. "I'm not really hungry."

"But you're so skinny," she says, as if this should suddenly inspire me to start grabbing food and stuffing it in my mouth.

"You're not, like, anorexic, are you?" The girl who's spoken is the one who is sitting directly across from me, a tall redhead who doesn't have room to talk about anyone being anorexic. She's like Mary-Kate Olsen, except nine inches taller.

"Emmylou!" Sophie looks horrified. "You can't just ask somebody you just met if they're anorexic." She looks back at me and lowers her voice conspiratorially. "You're not, are you?"

I can't help it; I burst out laughing. "No, but what makes

you think I'd tell you if I was? I just met you guys."

"Yeah, Sophie," pipes up the dark-headed girl sitting next to Emmylou. She gives me a pointed look. "We don't even know her." In contrast to Emmylou, she's really, really short— probably barely five feet—and her dark hair is cut in a chin-length bob. She looks sort of like an elf, but not necessarily in a bad way.

"So?" interjects the blond, athletic-looking girl on the other side of Sophie. "People go on national television and tell the entire world their deepest, darkest secrets. I'm Carly, by the way," she says, waving a carrot at me. "And that's Kate." She points the carrot at the elf.

"Uh, nice to meet you."

"Yeah, you too," she says, biting the top of the carrot.

Sophie gestures toward the carrot. "So today is orange, huh?"

"Yep." Carly reaches into her bag and pulls out the rest of her lunch, which consists of an orange and a plastic container filled with what looks like orange applesauce. "Carrots, an orange, and mashed sweet potatoes," she informs us, pointing at each thing. "Tomorrow is green—I'm thinking broccoli, grapes, maybe some spinach."

"Carly follows the color diet," Sophie explains, noticing my confused expression. "You assign each day a color, like green or orange, and then you only eat fruits and vegetables that are the color of the day."

"I have to get a wide range of nutrients so that my body functions at its optimal level for sports," Carly adds. Her voice is slightly defiant, as if she's expecting me to say something critical. I suppress the urge to laugh. Oh, if she only knew! Like I said earlier, I grew up with Daddy's parade of actress-model girlfriends who were ALL on some kind of freako diet. The grapefruit diet, the carrot juice diet, the coffee and cigarettes diet, the cocaine diet—Carly will have to come up with something WAY more bizarre than monochromatic food if she wants to shock me.

"Cool," I say.

"Yeah," Carly agrees awkwardly, clearly surprised by my ready acceptance. She pauses as if trying to think of something else to say to me, but then abandons that idea and turns to Emmylou.

"Hey, Em, can I borrow your algebra book?"

It seems like an innocent question, but Emmylou immediately looks pissed. "Don't tell me you've already lost your—"

I can only understand snatches of the rest because they both start trying to talk over each other, but I manage to discern that Emmylou has issues with Carly's organizational skills, while Carly feels that Emmylou has a "stick up her ass."

"So, how was your morning?" Sophie asks, turning to me as if Emmylou and Carly aren't even there. "Were your classes okay?"

"Uh—they were all right," I answer her, eyeing Emmylou and Carly warily. I'd like to ask Sophie more about sewing and her mom's store and everything, but it's kind of hard to carry on a conversation with them having World War III right next to us.

I turn away from them, intending to focus all my attention on talking to Sophie, but instead I find myself involuntarily scanning the crowded cafeteria for Steven. Okay. Fine. I admit it. I AM in lust with him. And, really, is there anything wrong with that? I mean, I need some sort of distraction if I'm going to make it through this ordeal.

Just like in the auditorium, though, I don't see him anywhere. "Do you know a guy named Steven Kinney?" I ask Sophie, mentally thanking the principal for supplying me with Steven's last name.

Sophie opens her mouth to respond, but suddenly Carly's voice rises shrilly above the din of cafeteria noise. "At least my boyfriend didn't break up with me because I spend all my time with a stupid horse!"

Sophie slaps her palm down in the middle of the table between them. "That's enough!" she scolds them. "You two stop it right now."

I expect them to ignore her since Sophie is, like, the most nonthreatening person ever, but to my surprise, they both shut up. They look chastised, even.

"All right," Carly mumbles, taking a vicious bite out of one of her carrots. Emmylou nods.

"Good." Sophie withdraws her hand and turns back to me. "Now, what was it you were asking me?"

"Er—" I begin hesitantly. Now that Emmylou and Carly aren't arguing, all four of them are looking at me.

Sophie snaps her fingers. "Oh yeah, Steven Kinney. Sure I know him. Everybody knows him."

"Everybody knows *everybody* here," Carly says wryly. She's finished the carrots and is now peeling the orange. "It's not exactly a big school."

"Plus, Steven is super-hot," Emmylou puts in.

"Yeah, but he's, like, totally bad news," Kate counters. She looks at me even more suspiciously. "How do you know him?"

"I don't. We just sort of bumped into each other this morning," I reply truthfully, deciding to omit the part where we live in the same house and I almost had sex with him yesterday. "So what's his deal?" I ask nonchalantly, even though I'm dying to know what sort of scandalous behavior has caused Kate to label him "bad news."

Sophie shrugs. "He's a typical bad boy. You know — parties a lot, cuts class, and generally manages to—"

"Sophie! Here you are." Three girls with identical blond hair extensions suddenly come up behind Sophie's chair and interrupt her.

The middle girl bends down and squeezes Sophie's shoulders in a hug. "I've been looking all over for you."

"Hey," Sophie mumbles, obviously less than thrilled at being found. Across the table I notice Emmylou and Carly exchange a dark look. Apparently they're not thrilled about this girl finding Sophie either. I'm not too happy about it myself, considering Sophie was in the middle of telling me about Steven.

"So have you thought about my offer?" the girl asks Sophie. All three girls are wearing identical tight, white T-shirts with POSSUM GRAPE CHEER airbrushed in pink across the front.

Now Sophie turns. "I'm sorry, Jaci. I just don't have time.

You know, with school and helping out at the store and all."

"Oh." The girl's face falls. "Are you sure?"

Sophie nods. "I'm just too busy."

"Well, okay," the girl replies reluctantly. "See you later, then." She leaves, the others trailing her.

As soon as they're gone, Kate, Emmylou, and Carly all start peppering Sophie with questions at the same time. Apparently I'm not the only one with no idea of what just happened. Sophie holds up her hands. "Okay, okay. Shut up so I can talk."

They all fall silent and stare at Sophie expectantly.

"It's not a big deal," she tells them, glancing around the table. "Jaci asked me to make her a dress, but as you just heard, I told her no."

"That *bitch*," Carly exclaims. "I can't believe she had the gall to ask you that."

"Me neither," Emmylou agrees.

"For some reason I get the idea you guys don't like that girl," I say jokingly. "Who is she, anyway?" I add.

Sophie blows out a breath. "Her name is Jaci Burton. And the two girls who were with her are Megan Pinter and Allison Wells."

"And we don't like them because . . ." I expect them all to start talking at the same time again, but Sophie is the only one who answers.

"Oh, you know," she says, making a vague gesture with her hand. "They think they're better than everybody else because they're cheerleaders, blah, blah, blah. Typical stuff."

The afternoon passes slower than the morning, if that's possible. By the time I get to algebra, my last class, it's like time is actually moving backward instead of forward.

Fortunately, however, the algebra teacher turns out to be one of those distracted, crazy-professor types who probably wouldn't notice if half the class was suddenly kidnapped by aliens, so I figure I can pass some of the time by texting Delaney.

She STILL hasn't called me, which I can't believe. I mean, she's never blown me off like this, not even when we were thirteen and Alice made her go to a therapy group for "troubled" teens after I talked her into taking her dad's Porsche for a joy ride.

Hunching over so that my hair falls forward to conceal what I'm doing, I tap out a short message.

911! CALL ME ASAP!!

I put in Delaney's number and hit send. There, I think, leaning back. That should get her attention. Unlike a lot of people, I don't 911 very often, so Delaney will realize it's important.

As soon as I sit back, somebody taps me on the shoulder. Surprised, I turn around. Besides Sophie and her friends, only one person has spoken directly to me the entire day (not counting Steven and the principal) and that was an awestruck-looking girl who asked me if I was really Paris Hilton. It's an understandable mistake, actually, because Paris and I DO have a lot in common. Well, except for the sex tape thing. And the fact that I'm not a moron.

The tapper turns out to be the guy I saw walking with Clint this morning in the auditorium.

He points to my phone. "You're not allowed to do that in class." The superior smirk on his face reminds me annoyingly of Clint, and I have no trouble picturing them as friends.

I stare at him, incredulous. What is he, the freaking room monitor or something?

"It's not allowed," he says again, more slowly this time, as if maybe I didn't understand him.

I give him a disgusted look and turn around without answering, but he starts tapping me AGAIN. I whirl around. "What!" I hiss.

"You can't do that in class," he tells me for what is now the third time. "I'm going to have to tell on you."

Tell on me? Are we in kindergarten or something? I grab my purse off the back of the chair, yank it open and, with an exaggerated motion, drop the phone inside. "Satisfied?"

He exhales loudly, clearly aggrieved by my rule breaking. "Fine. I'll let it go this time, but if it happens again, I'm telling immediately."

Lucky for Mr. Tattletale, the dismissal bell rings at that moment because my first urge is to retrieve the phone from my purse and hit him upside the head with it. If I'm going to get in trouble, it might as well be for something worthwhile, and knocking the crap out of this guy would practically be a public service.

Instead of assaulting him, though, I force myself to turn around and gather up my things. Keeping my gaze firmly ahead in case Mr. T is walking behind me, I join the line of people streaming out of the classroom into the hall. People are laughing and talking animatedly, the afternoon doldrums replaced by the excitement of freedom. I allow the crowd to buffet me along, in no hurry whatsoever to follow Sherri's instructions to meet Clint by the front doors when school was over. I assume that's where she's going to pick us up, since that's where she dropped us off this morning. Joy. Another ride in the minivan.

The tide of people eventually carries me through a set of double doors leading outside to the student parking lot, which is located in the back of the school. Unlike the parking lot at my school in L.A., which looks like a BMW dealership, PG High's is filled with regular-looking cars and, of course, a healthy number of pickup trucks. I watch the students as they climb into their vehicles, wondering why Clint doesn't have a car. Sherri told me the driving age here is sixteen, so I know he's old enough. Will Sherri and Joe not buy him one? Or does Clint think being chauffeured around in his mom's minivan is cool?

I follow the sidewalk around to the front of the school, dreading being enclosed with Clint and Sherri, but as I round the corner, I'm met not with a line of mom cars, but a line of buses. Big yellow buses. And pacing alongside one of them, looking pissed off as usual, is Clint.

I freeze. Oh, no. No, no, no, no. No way am I getting on one of those things. The minivan is bad enough, but at least I'll eventually be able to block it from my mind; I'll be scarred forever if I have to ride on a big, yellow school bus.

Slowly, I force my feet to move. I have no desire to get any closer to the yellow monstrosities, but I have to tell Clint that I'm not accompanying him home.

"You're late," he informs me as soon as I reach him.

I ignore the reprimand. "I can't ride a bus," I tell him.

"Why not?"

"Because—" I stare helplessly at the big, yellow bus, trying to think of an answer that won't make me sound like a total diva. "I . . . have a phobia," I say finally.

"A phobia," he repeats. "Of buses."

I nod. "Why do we have to ride a bus, anyway?" I ask, eager to change the topic away from my bus phobia. "Why don't you have a car or a truck or something?"

"Gee, I don't know," he says sarcastically. "Maybe because my mom made me sell the truck my dad bought me because she said it wasn't fair for me to have a vehicle if they couldn't afford to buy one for my stupid cousin too."

"That sucks," I say sympathetically. "I bet you hate your cousin."

He gives me a weird look. "Yeah, I do."

I start to nod, and then understanding dawns. OMG, *I'm* the stupid cousin. "Sherri made you sell your truck because of *me*?" I ask, flabbergasted.

"Duh, that's what I just said, isn't it? Thanks to you, I'm the only junior who still has to ride the bus like a little kid. Just because my mom was worried you might *feel bad*."

"But I have two cars," I blurt, because, apparently, I AM stupid. Good job, West. Be sure and mention that your dad lets you drive his cars, too. All eight of them.

"Well, isn't that just peachy," he says, yanking his backpack off the ground. "All I have is a friggin ten-speed." He slings his backpack over his shoulder and starts walking toward the bus.

"Clint, wait!" I call lamely. He doesn't, of course. He walks to the bus and gets on without so much as a glance back. Not that I blame him, really. I mean, no wonder the guy hates me. His mom made him sell his truck because of me! That's definitely hate-worthy, specially since it was for such a crazy reason. Sherri was worried I might be jealous of Clint? That's like worrying Angelina Jolie might be jealous of Kathy Griffin for being prettier than she is.

The bus starts pulling away from the curb, and I'm struck by a sudden uneasiness. What am I going to do now? I was so focused on avoiding the potential trauma of riding it that I didn't consider how I was actually going to get back to Sherri's house. The bus is still barely moving and for a fleeting moment I consider running after it, but I quickly exterminate that idea. I'm NOT riding on a yellow school bus. I'm not. I'll take a cab back to Sherri's. Except I'm pretty sure there isn't a cab service in Possum Grape. And walking is out of the question since Sherri's house is, like, a gajillion miles away from the school.

"West! Hey, West!"

I glance up at the sound of my name. It's like a scene from a movie when the heroine narrowly escapes the jaws of death thanks to a perfectly timed rescue by the hero. Sophie is waving at me from behind the wheel of a battered VW Bug convertible painted with an astonishing array of psychedelic flowers. *Sophie!* I think gratefully, moving toward her. *She'll take me home!*

I'm so relieved, I barely even glance at the wild paint job as

I walk over to her window. Kate is in the passenger's seat, an annoyed look on her face.

"What are you doing?" Sophie asks, peering at me over the rims of her heart-shaped sunglasses.

I glance back to the bus line, which is now almost empty. "Uh, I sort of missed the bus," I lie. Well, it's not really a lie, per se. I DID miss it, after all. So what if it was intentional?

"I can take you home," Sophie offers, just the way I hoped she would.

Sophie's generosity apparently displeases Kate, who gives me a fierce scowl.

"We were going to go to my mom's store for a little while," Sophie continues, oblivious to Kate. "Do you want to come, or do you have to get home right away?"

"No, I don't have to be back right now," I say, ignoring Kate. I grasp the door handle. "I'd love to go to your mom's store."

11
A Forrest Gump Secret Revealed

JoLynn's Fabrics is located in what Sophie informs me is the "old" downtown of PG, though how it earned that label I have no idea since the rest of the town looks exactly the same age: ancient.

Sophie parks "Buggy" in a space right by the front door, in front of a parking meter with an out-of-order sign taped to it.

"Um, I think the meter's broken," I tell Sophie as we pile out onto the sidewalk, thinking she hadn't noticed the sign.

Sophie laughs. "It's not broken," she says, flipping up the sign and putting a quarter in the slot. "G. W. just has a thing about hanging up signs." She points down the sidewalk. "See?"

I follow her finger. Four spaces down is a little man wearing what looks like a half dozen sweaters, even though it's sweltering outside. As we watch, he methodically tapes a sign to the meter and moves on to the next space.

"Won't he get in trouble?" I ask her, still watching him.

Sophie shakes her head. "Nah. He's been doing it for years. He puts them on Coke machines too."

After the water in the auditorium, I know I probably shouldn't bother saying anything, but I can't help myself. "And he does this because . . ."

Sophie frowns as if this question has never occurred to her before. "I don't know, maybe because—"

"The wheel's still turning, but the hamster is dead," Kate supplies dryly.

Sophie gives her a reproachful look. "I was going to say because he's a bit touched, but . . ." She shrugs her shoulders and pulls open the door to the store.

The first thing I see is a woman who could be Sophie's identical twin standing behind a long table cutting fabric from a bolt.

"Hi, Mama," Sophie says, going to peck her twin on the cheek.

"Hi, Ms. JoLynn," Kate says politely, which is probably quite a sacrifice considering it requires her to stop shooting daggers at me with her eyes for a moment.

Sophie takes my arm and pulls me toward her mom. "This is my new friend, West," she says proudly. "She just moved here from California. West, this is my mom, JoLynn."

Still cutting the fabric, JoLynn glances up to give me a quick once-over. On closer inspection, you can see the telltale signs that identify her as Sophie's mother rather than sister—she has the beginnings of fine lines at the corners of her eyes and around her mouth, as well as on her forehead. And, unlike Sophie with her bubbly, open personality, JoLynn seems reserved, almost guarded. "You're Crystal's daughter, aren't you?" she says absently, looking back down at her scissors.

"Y-yes," I say, startled at hearing my mother's name.

JoLynn lays the scissors down and starts folding the cut fabric into a neat square. "I thought so. You're the spitting image of her. You even sound a little bit like her."

"You knew my mother?" The question comes out sounding surprised, even though—duh—this IS the town where my mother grew up. Of course there are people here who knew her.

JoLynn nods. "She was a year behind me in school, but we rode the same bus."

My mom rode the school bus? I try to imagine my glamorous mother stepping onto a yellow school bus, but it's just too incomprehensible. I get the same uneasy feeling in my stomach that I did when Sherri and I were in the sunroom. I don't like people saying things that contradict my image of my mother.

"Wow, that's so cool," Sophie exclaims. "Our moms were friends!"

"We weren't really friends," her mom says quickly. "We just knew each other from the bus."

Sophie ignores the distinction. "See?" she says, hugging me. "Our meeting in the bathroom today was destiny."

Over Sophie's shoulder, I can see Kate rolling her eyes.

"West is a designer," Sophie tells her mom, releasing me.

JoLynn raises her eyebrows. "Oh, really?" Her tone is polite, but she's obviously less than impressed. No doubt she thinks I'm one of those rich girls who gets her parents to buy her a fashion line so she can run around and pretend like she has some sort of talent. Ever since Nicky Hilton came out with *Chick*, rich girls everywhere are trying to jump on the designer bandwagon.

Oblivious to her mother's skeptical look, Sophie motions for me to follow her. "Come on," she says excitedly. "I want to show you the dress I'm working on for the homecoming dance." She leads me to the back of the store and into a small, cramped workroom. Kate follows on my heels; I can practically feel her scathing stare boring into the back of my head.

Sophie is fussing with something in the corner—presumably the dress—but I can't get a good look at it because her back is turned, blocking my view. Kate straddles one of the wooden chairs, tapping her foot impatiently. I, on the other hand, couldn't care less if Sophie took all night. I figure the longer I'm here, the less of the evening I'll be at Sherri's.

Finally, Sophie turns around.

"Ta-da!" She plunks a dressmaker's dummy down in front of me with a flourish.

I blink, momentarily stunned. Although I was really impressed with Sophie's top this morning, I was honestly expecting her dress for the dance to be cute but basically uninspiring—a shift in a cool print, or maybe a little spaghetti strap number. Instead, the dummy is swathed in a stunning black and cream halter dress in a bold graphic print. Like Sophie's top, the dress shows excellent workmanship, with the halter straps extending from a cool black shell that looks like a necklace, a gathered bust, and ruching along the side seams. The length is fairly conservative—just below the knees—and the hem is a handkerchief, one of my favorites. I walk around to study the ruching down the back.

"So what do you think?"

I glance up, surprised to see that Sophie is wringing her hands nervously. It's the first time I've seen her less than 100 percent bubbly in our entire eight-hour relationship. "I love it," I tell her sincerely.

Her face brightens. "Really? You think it's okay?"

"Okay?" I laugh. "Sophie, this dress is fabulous. You're super talented." Out of the corner of my eye I see Kate's face relax a little. *Is that why she's been watching me like a hawk?* I wonder, incredulous. *Because she's afraid I'll say something mean to Sophie?* I immediately feel offended. Even if Sophie brought out the most hideous outfit in the world, I wouldn't TELL her it was the most hideous outfit in the world. Contrary to Sherri's opinion, I actually have had some "moral guidance." Sure, there are girls to whom I give the complete bitch treatment, but that's generally a "kill or be killed" situation. I would never be a bitch to somebody like Sophie who has been nothing but nice to me. I'm not a snot.

"It's really pretty," Kate echoes, even though based on her blah jeans and T-shirt, it's pretty obvious she's hardly qualified to give an opinion on anything fashion related.

"Of course I didn't design it," Sophie chatters happily, back to her old self now that she knows I like it. "I copied it."

"Really? From where?"

She goes to the table and riffles through a sheaf of haphazardly stacked magazine clippings. She pulls out a crumpled picture toward the back and hands it to me. It's a picture of Charlize Theron at a movie premiere wearing a dress that looks exactly like the one on Sophie's dummy.

"Sophie! I thought you said you couldn't sew without a pattern."

"I can't." She frowns, taking the picture back from me.

"Well how did you make this dress, then?"

She slides the picture back into the stack. "I looked at the picture, then made a pattern out of newspaper."

"That's pretty much the same thing."

She shakes her head. "No, it's not. I mean, sure, I can see a dress like this and copy it, but I could have never come up with it on my own. I'm not creative like that."

I'm pretty sure she's underestimating herself, but Arielle says it's not a good idea to pressure people until you're sure they're ready, so I let the comment about her un-creativity pass for now. "Well, ABS would certainly die to have you," I say, running my hand down the dress's skirt.

Kate frowns. "What's ABS?"

"A company that makes inexpensive copies of dresses that stars wear on the red carpet," Sophie says, beaming. "Do you want to see some of the other stuff I've made?" she asks me excitedly. "Mama takes pictures of everything."

I nod eagerly. It's totally cool to finally meet a girl my age who likes to sew. And, like I said, I'm grateful for anything that delays my return to Sherri's house.

Sophie dashes out of the room. Kate glances at me and quickly follows. Obviously the thought of being left alone with me is too much to bear.

A few minutes later, Sophie returns with a big, black photo album clutched to her chest. She sweeps a pile of scrap material off the worktable with her arm, then places the album in the newly cleared spot. "Come on," she says excitedly, pulling two folding chairs up to the table. "This is going to be so fun."

"What about Kate?" I ask, moving to sit in one of the chairs. "Doesn't she want to see too?"

"Hardly." Sophie laughs. "She's been tortured with it many, many times before. She left to go to her dad's garage. It's not very far from here."

"Oh. By any chance did one of her parents force her to sell her car because of me?"

"*What?*" Sophie laughs. "Are you hallucinating?"

"Well, Clint and Kate both hate me, and I just discovered that the reason Clint hates me is because his mom made him sell his truck because she couldn't afford to buy me a vehicle too. So I wondered if maybe Kate's parents had done the same thing."

"Kate doesn't hate you." Sophie waves her hand dismissively. "That's just her personality."

"Her personality is to act like she hates everyone?"

Sophie shakes her head. "She doesn't hate everyone. That's just her—what's it called?—protective mechanism."

"Her 'protective mechanism'?" I repeat. "What exactly is she protecting herself from?"

Sophie's expression becomes suddenly serious. "Look, I'll

tell you why Kate's like she is, but you have to swear you'll never ever say anything about it."

"O-okay," I stammer, even though I'm not certain I really *want* Sophie to tell me about Kate. What if it's some big, dark secret, like she's being abused or something? I mean, I did just meet these girls a few hours ago.

Sophie glances around the room as if checking to make sure Kate didn't slip back in when we weren't paying attention. Satisfied, she turns back to me. "Okay, it's like this. When we were younger, Kate had something wrong with her legs. Her feet turned in like this." She pushes her chair back and turns her feet inward until the toes of her shoes touch to demonstrate.

"That's terrible," I say, shocked.

"I know." She releases her feet into their normal position and pulls her chair back up to the table. "She had some kind of surgery to fix them when she was a baby, but it didn't work or something—I'm not really sure what happened." She takes a deep breath. "Anyway, when we were little, Kate had to wear these big, metal braces on her legs. You know, like in that movie, *Forrest Gump*?" She falls silent, and I realize she's waiting for me to acknowledge that I've seen *Forrest Gump*.

"Uh, yeah. When Forrest is little he has braces on his legs and all the kids tease him."

"Exactly," Sophie says. "And that's what happened to Kate, too."

"She had to wear the leg braces to school?" I ask, aghast. "I thought you meant she had leg braces when she was, like, three or four years old or something."

Sophie's expression is sorrowful. "She didn't get them off until we were in sixth grade. And by that time, it was too late. Her legs and feet were normal, but she'd endured so many years of teasing that her spirit was just destroyed."

"Oh, Sophie, that's *terrible*." A pang of sympathy squeezes my heart as I picture Kate as a little girl with her legs weighted down by clunky braces.

"So you see," Sophie continues, "it's not that Kate has anything against you *personally*. It's just that she's seen the worst people have to offer—so much so that now she just assumes everyone is awful, whether it's justified or not."

"She obviously doesn't think you're awful," I point out. "Or Emmylou and Carly."

Now Sophie smiles. "That's because we're the only people who stood up for her back then. One time we were at the park and this boy kept singing this song—G-I-M-P spells gimp— and Carly bloodied his nose, even though he was two years older than we were."

I think about Carly's cut bicep and have no trouble picturing her giving someone a bloody nose. I shake my head. "Little kids are so mean to one another."

"Tell me about it," Sophie agrees. "That's actually the real reason why I told Jaci I couldn't make her an outfit."

"Because little kids are mean?" I say, confused.

"Because *Jaci* was a mean little kid," Sophie clarifies. "Of all the people who teased Kate when we were little, Jaci was the cruelest. Kate would be devastated if loaned her a pencil, much less made her an outfit."

I nod approvingly. If Maria were here, she'd probably say something like everyone deserves a second chance, especially since they were little kids and all that was so long ago, but I agree with Kate and Sophie. There are some things you just don't get over.

"So you're not going to say anything, right?" Sophie asks. "I mean, it's not like it's a secret that Kate had leg braces, but she'd be upset if she knew I told you about it."

"I won't say anything to anyone," I promise firmly.

12

Desperate Times Call for Desperate Workouts

I spend almost three hours at JoLynn's, chatting with Sophie and looking at her scrapbook. She wasn't kidding about her mom taking pictures of everything—her scrapbook is, like, one hundred pages long. It takes us more than an hour just to get through it. I don't mind, though. It's actually kind of nice to hang out with a "normal" person for a change. I even tell Sophie (albeit in much abbreviated detail) about the situation with my dad, Zane, and the party.

It's the most fun I've had since I got to Possum Grape, aside from my rendezvous with Steven. But all good things must come to an end, as I'm reminded when Sherri rushes out of the house as Sophie pulls up to drop me off.

As I step out of the car, she hurries down the steps and throws her arms around me. "Where have you been? I've been worried sick. Clint said you got mad and refused to get on the bus."

Of course he did. I gesture toward the car. "I've been with Sophie. We went to her mom's fabric store."

Sherri lets go of me and bends down to peer into the car. Her face lights up in a smile of recognition. "Sophie! How are you? How's your mom?"

"We're both fine, Mrs. Reynolds," Sophie says politely.

Sherri gestures toward Buggy. "Well, turn this thing off and come inside," she tells Sophie. "You can have dinner with us."

"Oh, I can't," Sophie says hastily. "I have to get back and help my mom. We're having a sale this weekend."

"Are you sure?" Sherri asks. "We're having fried catfish."

We're having catfish? *Catfish?* As in part cat, part fish?

Sophie shakes her head. "I can't. Mama would be mad."

"Okay, but you're missing out," Sherri tells her.

"I know," Sophie says apologetically, almost like she really IS sorry she can't stay to eat. She puts Buggy in gear and waves. "Bye, Mrs. Reynolds. Bye, West. See you at school tomorrow."

I watch Buggy disappear down the drive, wishing I was going back to JoLynn's too instead of inside to whatever culinary horror Sherri has waiting.

"I'm so happy you made a friend," Sherri exclaims, squeezing my arm. "And especially one like Sophie, who comes from a good, Christian family." She shakes her head regretfully. "It's too bad she couldn't stay for catfish, though."

Dinner is exactly what I expected: greasy and unrecognizable. The only saving grace is that I can't actually identify it as a fish, cat or otherwise. If the whole concept of forcing yourself to throw up wasn't totally twisted and gross, I'd seriously consider taking up bulimia on a temporary basis. Unfortunately, it IS twisted and gross. Plus, *Cosmo* did this whole article on how it can make your teeth yellow and fall out. That means I have only one other option if I still want to fit into my clothes when I get back to L.A.: exercise. Hardcore exercise.

"What are you doing?" Dakota is standing in the doorway of the bedroom staring at me with a mixture of awe and amazement.

"Abs," I gasp, straining as I lift my knees to my chest. Although bunk beds are useless in the comfort and sleep department, it turns out that, in a pickle, the top bunk is a remarkable substitute for a Roman Chair. Warning: Novices, people within a fifty-mile radius of an actual gym, or anyone with a Tae Bo video should not attempt this type of bunk-bed workout. The maneuvers discussed herein are the actions of a desperate woman.

Dakota wrinkles her nose. "What's 'abs'?"

I squeeze out my last two reps and drop to the ground. "It's short for abdomen." I go over to the desk and pick up the orange plastic glass filled with ice water I brought from the kitchen. (Sherri doesn't believe in bottled water.) "You know—your stomach." I point to the exposed patch of skin between the waistband of my pants and the bottom of my tank top. After a drink of water, I move to the center of the room and begin a set of backward lunges with my left leg.

Dakota immediately moves beside me and attempts to

imitate the movement. "Is this for your abs too?" she asks, her eyes trained on my left leg.

"A little," I pant. "Lunges are primarily for your hamstrings, quads, and glutes." I point to each muscle group as I say its name.

Dakota pauses mid-lunge and repeats the names to herself, as if committing them to memory. A surge of pride washes over me. Maybe the judge did have a point when she said having fake siblings would be an enriching experience, I realize suddenly. I could, like, totally shape Dakota's young mind.

After backward lunges, Dakota and I do forward lunges, side lunges, squats, calf raises, and roundhouse kicks. Dakota watches me intently the whole time, focused on copying each move exactly. And, thanks to being part Energizer Bunny, she's not even winded when we finally break for water.

"That was fun!" she says, dancing around me as I gulp my ice water. Even though I haven't been out of the gym for that long, I'm already feeling the effects. And although my stomach is still undeniably toned, it's *showing* the effects. The slight slackening probably isn't anything that anyone besides me and my trainer would notice, but it's there just the same. And while we're on the subject of workouts, let's take a moment to talk about celebrities. A lot of models and stars get a charge out of telling interviewers that they maintain their six-pack abs and J-Lo butt by "hiking in nature" or "chasing after their kids"or—my personal favorite—that they were "just blessed with good genetics," so I'd like to take this opportunity to set the record straight. THEY'RE LYING.

I'm not saying that they *don't* have good genetics and hike and chase their kids or whatever, but trust me—those things are definitely not the sum total of their workout regime. You don't get Madonna arms from pushing a three-year-old on the swings. You get them from working out three hours a day, the way Madonna does. And ADMITS to doing. I love Madge.

I hold out the glass of water to Dakota, but she shakes her head. Clearly there's some camel mixed in with the Energizer Bunny genetics. "Are we going to do more exercises?" she asks hopefully.

"Well, we still need to do upper body," I tell her, draining the last of the water. "But to get the most benefit, we need to use some kind of weight." Although my lower body is relatively easy to tone and maintain, my arms and chest require serious strength training. I put down the empty glass and survey the room critically, looking for something to use as free weights. Stuffed animals? No, way too light. The Barbie House in the corner is probably heavy enough, but it's also a Barbie House. I'm about to abandon the idea and just tell Dakota we'll do it without anything when I suddenly remember the free weights in Steven's room.

"I know something we can use," I tell Dakota. "Wait here and I'll be right back." Psyched at the idea of actually using real equipment, I bound out of the room and head toward the rickety stairs that lead to the second floor. Okay, so I'm also a little psyched about seeing Steven, assuming he's even in his room and not out doing whatever it is he does when he's being invisible.

This time when I emerge onto the second-floor landing,

there's no smell of marijuana. If Steven is in his room, he's behaving himself.

When I push open the door, I discover that not only is he behaving himself, he's doing his homework.

"What are you doing?" I ask, surprised to see him sitting on the floor with papers spread out around him.

He makes a show of checking the cover of the book in his hand. "Hmmm. According to this, something called calculus."

Mr. HNG does calculus? I sort of figured him as the all body and no brains type. Which was totally judgmental of me. Bad West. "Oh." I try to look nonchalant, like it would have been totally shocking to find him doing anything *other* than calculus.

Steven isn't fooled. "I don't just smoke pot up here, you know." He smiles and sets the book down on the floor beside him, the perfect Abercrombie & Fitch model-scholar.

Oh, God. I have to get out of here QUICK, before I do something I'll regret. I walk over to the free weights so I don't have to look at him. "I just came up here to, um, see if I could borrow these," I tell him, reaching down to pick up the pair of fifteen-pound dumbbells. "To work out with," I add stupidly. Duh, West. What else would he think you were going to do with them—paint your nails?

"Sure. Whatever. You can take the others, too, if you want." He gestures toward the three sets of dumbbells that are still on the floor.

"That's okay," I answer, already backing toward the door. "Those are too heavy."

"You know what you can handle." He shrugs and reaches for his calculus book. I turn to go, relieved that I managed not to do anything stupid, but then, impulsively, I spin back around. "Look, Steven, about what happened the other day—"

"It's no big deal," he interrupts, not looking up from his calculus book. "Forget about it."

I open my mouth to say something else, but I close it when I realize I don't have anything to say. I don't even know why I felt the need to bring it up in the first place, except that in between knocking him in the head with the bathroom door and being busted by the principal, I never really got the chance to apologize again.

"Okay, then. Well, see you later," I say awkwardly.

"Later," he echoes absently, leaning over to scribble something on a piece of paper.

Leaving him to be smart and gorgeous alone, I balance the dumbbells on my shoulders and pick my way carefully down the stairs. As I emerge onto the first floor, I glance up just in time to see Clint passing by. As usual, he's engrossed in his Game Boy (*what* is so freaking interesting about that thing?), so he doesn't notice me. I sigh. It's so tempting to just go back to Dakota's room and continue my workout, but now that I know about Sherri and the truck thing, I feel obligated to try to talk to him about it.

"Clint," I call out, hurrying toward him.

Startled, he glances up from his Game Boy and turns around to see who is talking to him. When he realizes it's me, he tries to turn back around and keep going, but it's too late; I've already caught up to him.

"What do *you* want?" he says meanly. "Did you chase me down to tell me more about your two cars?"

Okay. I deserved that, I guess. I suck in a breath. "Look, Clint, about that—I just wanted to tell you that I'm SO sorry your mom made you sell your truck because of me." I readjust the dumbbells on my shoulders. "Really, I am. I know she meant well and everything, but it was still a shitty thing to do. And I don't blame you for resenting me because of it," I finish earnestly.

I catch the naked look of surprise in his eyes before he averts his gaze. "Yeah, well," he says uncomfortably, fiddling with his Game Boy. "You're right. It was a shitty thing to do. I bailed hay for three summers so I could buy that truck," he adds.

Great. Like I don't feel bad enough. Next he'll tell me he sold one of his kidneys too. And the really unfair thing is that it's NOT EVEN MY FREAKING FAULT Sherri made him get rid of his stupid truck. It's not like I *told* her to do it or any-thing. Sherri just seems to have a special talent for coming up with crazy, misguided ideas and then acting on them. Like how she thinks my mom is counting on her to save my soul.

Still, it's understandable why the whole thing wouldn't exactly make Clint feel warm and fuzzy toward me, I remind myself.

"I'm really sorry," I repeat. "I'm going to talk to your mom about it first thing tomorrow."

"No!" He jerks his head up from the Game Boy. "That's not a good idea."

"Why not? I'll just tell her that it was a thoughtful thing to do but totally unnecessary. Then she'll let you get another truck. Right?"

He shakes his head. "My mom doesn't work like that. Once she's made up her mind about something, that's it. She won't budge."

"But she made up her mind on the basis of an incorrect assumption," I argue. "She has to budge." Just like how she has to budge on the whole me-living-here thing, I add silently.

"You obviously don't know my mom," he replies dryly.

"I guess not."

Great, I think cynically as I turn to go back to Dakota's room. Sherri's insane AND irrationally stubborn. Getting back to L.A. should be as painless as a Brazilian bikini wax.

13
Extreme Makeover: Kate Edition

In keeping with my idea about molding Dakota, I decide to give her an education in fashion by making her a new wardrobe. What better way to teach her good taste than by outfitting her in it? Plus, she really needs some new clothes. I mean, it's not like she looks like a street urchin or anything, but she could definitely use some more stuff—things I know Sherri can't afford.

When I mention my plan to Sophie the next day at lunch, she immediately insists on helping, so as soon as school lets out, I go back to JoLynn's with her and Kate. Kate's attitude toward me hasn't improved one iota, even though I'm being super nice to her. If anything, it seems like the more effort I make, the more she dislikes me.

"How are you going to pay for all that?" she asks Sophie sourly, gesturing to the half dozen bolts of material we've piled on the worktable. Sophie is sitting beside the material, study-ing a short set I sketched during study hall. "I haven't thought about it," she murmurs absently.

"You surely don't expect your mother to just give it to you for free." Kate's supposedly addressing Sophie, but it's clear this statement is really meant for me.

"I would never take advantage of JoLynn like that," I assure Kate. "I'll pay for anything we use out of my trust fund." I realize, belatedly, how spoiled that probably sounds, but it's too late; the words have already left my mouth.

Sophie glances up from my sketch. "You have a trust fund?" she says, her eyes shining with amazement. "That is SO awesome. You're just like Paris and Nicky Hilton." OMG, will people please stop bringing up Paris Hilton?

"What's so awesome about it?" Kate scowls. "It's not like they worked for the money or anything. Trust-fund babies are just spoiled brats who think they can do whatever they want because their daddies are rich." She slants me a disgusted look to make certain I know she's referring to me, in case I'm—I don't know—THE STUPIDEST PERSON ON EARTH?

Even though I know Kate's psychologically damaged, I have to bite my tongue to keep from making some kind of nasty response. I mean, I feel really bad about everything she's been through, but I have feelings too, you know.

And then suddenly it occurs to me that if I'm helping Dakota grow as a person, maybe there's a way I can help Kate grow too. Maybe I could set up a phone session with Arielle or get her some books on meditation, or maybe I could give her . . . a makeover. Yes! A makeover!! That's EXACTLY what Kate needs, I realize excitedly. A good old-fashioned makeover.

Spare me the sarcastic comments. You know you love them. And what better way to show her that she's not the same little kid everybody bullied than to make her look like a brand-new person?

I move toward her, a plan rapidly forming in my head. "You know, Kate, has anybody ever told you that you look a lot like Natalie Portman?"

Kate gives me a startled glance. "Queen Amidala?"

God, she doesn't even know who Natalie Portman is. "No, Natalie Portman," I say slowly, clearly enunciating each syllable. "She's a famous actress."

"Queen Amidala is the name of the character Natalie Portman plays in Star Wars," Sophie tells me, her expression amused. "You know, the new ones? Kate's obsessed."

"Oh." I try to think of some Star Wars related quip, but all I can come up with is "May the force be with you," which doesn't seem appropriate to the moment. Truthfully, I don't know anything about the new Star Wars. I vaguely remember Delaney dragging me to one of them, but I think I fell asleep.

"I don't look like Natalie Portman," Kate says finally, shaking her head. "You're just trying to make me feel good."

"No, I'm not," I lie. "You really do look like her." Actually, that part isn't a lie. She does look like Natalie Portman, or at least the way Natalie Portman would look if she was pissed off all the time.

"No, I don't," she repeats, but this time there's the tiniest note of hesitancy in her voice.

I decide to take advantage of her uncertainty and give her the full-court press. "I can prove it to you, if you want."

She narrows her eyes suspiciously. "How can you do that?"

"Oh, you know." I make a careless movement with my hand. "A little makeup, a new outfit."

"You mean like a makeover?" She makes a face. "Those are stupid."

"No, they're not." Sophie flicks me a knowing look and gets to her feet. Finally! She has a clue about what I'm trying to do here. I thought I was going to have to send her a certified letter or something.

She walks to Kate and takes her hand. "They're fun, Katy-did. C'mon, let us do it."

"No way," Kate says automatically, but there's no force behind her words. I can tell the idea of looking like Queen Ami-thingy is hard for her to resist.

I move beside Sophie so that we're a united front. "There are a lot of girls who would kill to look like Natalie Portman."

"Lots," Sophie echoes, nodding her head sagely.

In the end, Sophie's big-eyed angel stare does her in. "Fine," Kate heaves. "Whatever makes you happy."

Sophie lets out an ear-piercing squeal and starts jumping up and down in excitement, clutching Kate's hand. Kate just stands there, though one corner of her mouth does turn upward slightly.

"There's one condition," I add, once Sophie is through freaking out.

Their heads swivel toward me in unison, Kate's expression wary and Sophie's curious.

"What is it?" Sophie pants, out of breath.

"She has to wear her new look to school." I know. I'm evil. But what's the point of taking the trouble to make her over if nobody sees the new Kate except me and Sophie? Call me shallow, but I like my work to be admired. I wait for Kate to either tell me to go to hell or to back out of the whole thing, but to my surprise, she merely nods.

"Well, what are we waiting for?" Sophie exclaims. She shoves Kate unceremoniously into a chair.

"Give me a sec," I tell them. I go over to the stack of old magazines in the corner and start riffling through them, looking for a picture of Natalie Portman. The pile consists mostly of *People* and *Us*, so it doesn't take me too long to come up with a couple of photos—one of her in Sari Gueron and one of her in Chanel.

I'm about to turn away when a headline catches my eye. "Teen Queen Divorces Parents to Move to New York," an ancient issue of *Us* proclaims. Underneath the headline is a picture of a girl who was super hot three or so years ago, when she was, like, fifteen or sixteen, but then she just fell off the face of the earth. She does infomercials now, hawking some sort of space-age curling iron. Child Star 101: Invest your earnings. Your cuteness WILL wear off.

Despite her obvious stupidity, I'm intrigued by the title. I pick up the magazine and page through until I find the article.

Brooke Davenport, 16, the quirky, lovable star of last summer's sleeper hit, *Prom Queen*, was granted legal emancipation from her parents by a California judge last Thursday. The teen petitioned for emancipation after her parents refused to allow her to relocate from L.A. to New York in order to pursue "more serious" work on Broadway. Davenport's publicist declined to comment on the emancipation, but a source close to the actress says relations in the Davenport family remain amicable. "Brooke loves her parents very much, but she has a very independent spirit. She needs to be free to pursue her dreams."

I stop reading and simply rip the whole page out of the magazine. My heart is pounding so hard, I'm surprised Sophie and Kate can't hear it. Legal emancipation. Why in the world didn't I think of it before? If I'm legally emancipated, Sherri won't have any control over me. I'll be able to live wherever I want.

"Hey West, what do you think?"

I startle guiltily at the sound of Sophie's voice. Quickly, I shove the page inside my shirt and turn around.

Sophie has her hands on her hips, peering critically at Kate. "What do you think? I put eyeliner on her."

"Looks good," I reply automatically, not even glancing at Kate's eyelids. I can't think about eyeliner right now. All I can think about is how I HAVE to get a judge to declare me legally emancipated. I need to be free to pursue my dreams too, just like Brooke Davenport.

As long as I don't end up on an infomercial.

14

Saved! (and Not the Way I Want)

Although I specifically asked Sherri for permission to go to JoLynn's after school, when Sophie drops me off she comes rushing outside AGAIN.

"You're late," she exclaims, grabbing my hand and pulling me up the steps.

"I didn't know I was supposed to be home at a certain time," I reply breathlessly, trying not to stumble as she rushes me across the porch. What is her deal? Yes, I'm home a little later than yesterday because I worked on Dakota's clothes after Kate's makeover, but I'm not *that* late. And, like I said, I wasn't aware I had a curfew.

"Run to your room and put on that nice dress we got at Wal-Mart," she tells me, opening the screen door and ushering me through. "We've got just enough time to make it."

"Make it where?" I ask, confused. She never mentioned anything about going anywhere tonight.

"To church," she answers. "Reverend Billy decided to have an impromptu revival." She nudges me toward Dakota's room. "Hurry up and change now. Jesus doesn't like for people to be late."

Forty-five minutes later, I'm crammed in a pew between Clint and an old woman who has a bulging wad of tobacco in her cheek and a distinctive smell, listening to a man who very possibly escaped from a mental institution sometime in the recent past. Oh, yeah—and I'm wearing the grandma dress. In other words, it's a fabulous evening.

Reverend Billy bounces excitedly on the balls of his feet. "Do you feel the awesome Presence and Glory of the Lord here today?" he booms at the congregation. He extends the microphone out in front of him the way singers do when they want concertgoers to repeat a particular lyric.

Feverish responses of "Amen" ripple through the crowd. I have the urge to shout something nonsensical like "Go Lakers!" but I'm afraid I might get stoned to death or something. I'm not kidding; these people look *rabid*. Of the hundred or so people here, I'm the only one who isn't completely mesmerized by Reverend Billy. Sherri looks like she's about to have a freaking orgasm.

I shift uncomfortably in my three inches of seat space. I'm about to die from heat stroke in this dress. In addition to late people, Jesus apparently doesn't like air-conditioning, either, because this place is sweltering. Taking a cue from a pregnant woman a few rows up, I pick up the leaflet the usher gave me as we came into the church and fan myself as I resume gawking at the congregation.

Is this the way people in cults look—like zombies? I wonder as I futilely wave the flimsy paper in front of my face. Daddy dated a woman once who had been in a cult, and she was totally mental. I mean, outwardly, she was this really pretty, soft-spoken brunette, but she had these freaky, whispered conversations with herself—I'm talking LONG conversations—and then she started thinking people were talking to her through the radio. I'm not kidding; once when we were getting a pedicure together, a Coldplay song came on and she leaped out of her chair and screamed, "No, I forbid you!" Then she ran out of the salon with no shoes on and with cotton between her toes and everything.

After that, Daddy arranged for her to go to a "spa" for a couple of months, but then I never saw her again. What was her name, anyway? Something like Meredith or Michelle or—

"Aaargarmpf."

The old woman suddenly lurches into my side, interrupting my trip down memory lane. I instinctively shift in the opposite direction, thinking I must have inadvertently drifted over into her space, but her clawlike hand clamps down on my upper thigh. As her nails dig into my skin, her eyes roll back in her head and her body starts to quiver. Alarmed, I glance around frantically for somebody to help, but nobody else seems to have noticed.

Panicked, I prod Clint with my elbow. "Clint," I whisper urgently.

He doesn't respond. Like everyone else, he's totally caught up in whatever Reverend Billy is saying.

I ram my elbow into his ribs as hard as I can.

He jumps. "What is it?" he whispers, rubbing his side. Now that I've apologized for causing him to be without transportation, he's treating me like an actual human.

"Help me," I hiss. "This lady is having a seizure or something."

He glances at the old woman and back to me. "She's not having a seizure," he whispers, totally nonplussed. "She's being visited by the Holy Spirit." And with that helpful explanation, he returns his attention back to the front of the church.

I gape at his profile. *Visited by the Holy Spirit?* Is he freaking serious? I know about miracles and the Lord working in mysterious ways and all that, but I've never heard of—

The woman's eyes suddenly fly open and a rush of harsh, guttural sounds comes streaming out of her mouth.

With a shriek, I shove her off me and jump to my feet. A spirit is visiting her, all right, but I don't think it's a holy one.

She falls back against the pew, the strange sounds still coming out of her mouth, her body jerking like somebody is sending electric volts through it. I glance around, looking for help. Surely everybody can see that she needs an ambulance or an exorcism or something?

To my surprise, though, nobody seems to be looking at the possessed, old woman. Actually, people seem to be looking at me and . . . smiling? I do a double take. Why would they be smiling at me? I smile back uncertainly. Unless . . . this is, like, reality TV! Euphoria floods my body. That's it! This whole thing is some sort of elaborate hoax. Like, the longest episode of *Punk'd* ever made. Daddy's been threatening to do something like this for a couple of years, but I frankly thought I was too smart to be fooled. How totally like him to set it up while he's in prison, so I would never suspect.

I whirl around, looking for the cameras. I should be livid at Daddy for putting me through so much hell, but I'm too relieved to be mad. Sherri tugs on my dress. "Go on," she says, motioning toward the aisle. She gives me a broad smile. I smile back, instantly forgiving all of her psycho-bitch behavior. She was just doing what the producers told her to do, after all.

I step out of the pew into the aisle, still looking for the cameras. Reverend Billy beckons to me from up front. "Come up to the altar, young lady. Come up here and receive this experience."

Of course! Reverend Billy is the host of whatever this show is going to be called. I practically skip down the aisle toward the altar.

When I reach the altar, Reverend Billy holds out his hand and helps me up to stand beside him. I beam at the audience, determined to show that I'm a good sport.

Reverend Billy is still holding my hand. His palm is sweaty, but I'm too ecstatic even to be grossed out.

He faces me and speaks into his microphone. "Do you feel you've been touched by something special today, young lady?"

He holds the microphone under my mouth, and I nod enthusiastically. "Absolutely." Being on TV is pretty cool, after all, even if I am an unwitting participant.

He pulls the microphone back. "And are you ready to accept the awesome gift that the Higher Power wants to bestow on you?"

Calling the network a Higher Power is a little ostentatious, IMO, and I'm not sure I would classify a reality show as an "awesome gift," but whatever. I nod again. They're really milking the lead-up to the reveal moment for all it's worth.

He closes his eyes and puts his hand on my forehead. *Whoa,* I scream silently. Being on TV might be cool, but his sweaty hand touching my forehead is definitely not cool. I can practically feel the bacteria climbing into my pores, hoping to morph into a zit.

"Brothers and Sisters, let us give thanks to our sweet, loving Father for shining His light on this young lady today," he intones, his eyes still shut. "We welcome her into our church and pray that she doesn't stray from the divine path to Holy Salvation."

I feel my euphoria dissolving and the first frissons of alarm creeping up my spine. I was expecting him to break character and tell me this is all a joke, but he seems really serious. When I glance out at the congregation and see that they all have their heads bowed, my alarm amps up to full-fledged panic. This isn't a reality show; it's totally real. I'm standing in front of an entire church while a sweaty minister gives me forehead zits while praying about leading me to Holy Salvation.

My first instinct is to leap down from the altar and make a run for the door, but my legs stay firmly rooted to the spot, apparently having better sense than my brain. You can't just bail when somebody's saving your soul; that would be totally rude, right? I'm going to have to stand here until he's finished, even though tears are about to spill over my lashes. For one golden, fleeting moment, I thought I was going back to L.A., and now I'm on display at Sherri's weird church, feeling more disappointed than I ever thought possible.

Reverend Billy—who I guess is a real reverend and not a television host in disguise—drones on, praying for me to "embrace" my new life and thanking God for doing "spiritual surgery" on my soul. I listen halfheartedly, more concerned with trying to remember whether or not I brought my home microdermabrasion system with me from L.A. If I exfoliate and tone as soon as I get back to Sherri's, I can probably ward off any potential damage from his sweaty hand.

Finally, he opens his eyes and drops his hand. "Let's show this young lady our support, Brothers and Sisters," he declares, gesturing toward me. I smile weakly as applause breaks out, mingled with shouts of "Amen" and "Praise Jesus." I'm overcome by the ridiculous feeling that I should bow or curtsy or something.

I expect him to continue with the service after the clapping dies down, but apparently the rescue of my soul was the grand finale because Reverend Billy replaces the microphone on its stand and people start getting up from their seats. I look around hesitantly and step down from the altar, but that's as

far as I make it before people start rushing forward to con-
gratulate me. I shake hands in a flurry, smiling and making
unintelligible murmurs that I hope sound gracious. It's like I've
won a gold medal or something.

Dakota pushes her way through the cluster of people and
clutches my skirt, her face flushed with excitement. Sherri
appears behind her, dabbing at her eyes with a tissue. "I'm so
proud of you," she gushes, pulling me into a fierce hug. "I knew
you'd choose the right path if someone showed you the way."

Dakota, who has been watching us impatiently, tugs on my
skirt. "How did it feel?" she asks eagerly. "When the Holy
Spirit came over you?"

"Er—"

"Did you feel tingly and stuff?"

"Yeah, that's it," I say, relieved I don't have to come up with
my own lie. "Tingly. And stuff."

"I'm just so proud of you," Sherri repeats, tucking the used
tissue into her purse. She holds out her hands to me and
Dakota. "Come on, girls. I think this calls for a trip to the Sno-
Kone Shack."

In the perfect, surreal ending to this totally surreal evening,
we meet up with Joe and Clint and go to the wooden stand
across the street to order cherry Sno-Kones and celebrate my
salvation.

15

I'm a Sucker,
and Luke's a Jerk

"Who are you and what have you done with Kate?" Emmylou gapes at the newly transformed Kate.

"Shut up," Kate mumbles, opening her locker, but the pleased expression on her face is obvious. Despite our bargain, I half expected her to show up in her regular clothes, but she's actually wearing the outfit Sophie and I put together yesterday—a black and gold gypsy dress I made out of some leftover pieces of chiffon JoLynn gave me, worn over a pair of old jeans Sophie scrounged up and hemmed to fit Kate's five-one frame.

In keeping with the gypsy look, we went to the thrift shop on the other side of town and bought some necklaces and bracelets for her to layer. Sophie did her hair and makeup, which really wasn't a big deal (some gel, a little eye liner, and lipstick), but the effect is totally dramatic. I wouldn't be surprised if some people think she's a new student.

"Seriously, were you kidnapped by aliens or something?" Emmylou presses. "What happened to you?"

"We gave her a makeover!" Sophie squeals. "Doesn't she look great?"

"Fantastic," Emmylou murmurs, unable to stop staring. She reaches out and tentatively touches a strand of Kate's hair as if she can't believe she's actually real.

Kate is dangerously close to beaming, though she's fighting it with everything she's worth. If I wasn't so wrapped up in myself right now, I might actually feel a sense of pride or accomplishment or something, but I'm too busy obsessing about last night. I tug on Sophie's sleeve.

"So you're saying I've basically joined their cult?" I demand, continuing the conversation we were having before Emmylou and Kate arrived.

Initially, I thought the whole being "saved" thing was just another annoyance I had to endure, but after last night's celebratory Sno-Kones, I started worrying I might have gotten in over my head. Perhaps it had something to do with the way Sherri kept beaming at me and saying, "You're one of us now."

Sophie's brow wrinkles as she turns her attention away from Kate and back to me. "It's a church, West. 'Cult' sounds like they're cutting the heads off chickens or sacrificing virgins or something."

"Well, the woman beside me was possessed by a demon," I argue. "She was shaking and saying all this gibberish."

Sophie laughs. "She was speaking in tongues. Lots of people do it."

"Lots of idiots, you mean." Kate has shut her locker and is listening to our conversation. Emmylou gives a hurried wave and slips off down the hall, clearly eager not to be part of this particular conversation.

"That's not nice," Sophie scolds Kate. "Speaking in tongues is just a manifestation of some people's beliefs."

"Speaking in tongues is a type of mass-induced hysteria," Kate says flatly, unabashed. She glances between me and Sophie. "Whose been speaking in tongues, anyway?"

"The woman next to me at church," I answer.

"West got saved last night," Sophie adds.

Kate looks incredulous. "You? Got saved?" She starts to laugh.

"I don't see what's so funny," I say, annoyed. "I didn't know what was going on. They tricked me."

She stops and looks at me for a moment like she's going to say something, but then she just bursts out laughing again.

Okay. Now I'm REALLY annoyed. I did make her drab, dreary little butt over yesterday. The least she could do is follow proper etiquette and act sympathetic to my face and laugh later, behind my back. Not to mention that she, of all people, should know what's it's like to be made fun of.

"What's so funny?" Carly joins us, munching on what looks like a raw tomato.

"West got saved." Kate barely chokes the words out.

I narrow my eyes at her. This is getting ridiculous. I admit the whole thing has some humor value, but it's not THAT funny.

Carly looks at me, her eyes wide. "You did? How do you feel?"

Like I want to hit Kate in the face with your tomato, I think. "Tingly and stuff," I say aloud, borrowing from Dakota again. By now I'm too weary to even attempt to explain the whole being-under-duress aspect of my religious experience.

Carly nods. "That's exactly how I felt."

"You've been saved?" This surprises me for some reason.

Carly gives me a "duh" look. "Um, yeah. Pretty much everyone's been saved by the time they're eleven or so."

"*I* haven't been." Kate has finally managed to stop laughing, though she's still wiping tears from her eyes.

"That's because you're a heathen," Carly says good-naturedly, patting her on the shoulder. Unlike Emmylou, Carly seems not to have even noticed that Kate looks like a completely different person. Carly looks back at me. "Kate's a Wiccan," she explains. "You know, it's like witchcraft."

"No, it's not," Kate says defensively.

Sophie has been silent for the past several minutes, but now she cuts Kate off. "All right, all right. We've had this conversation, like, a thousand times, you guys. Drop it."

Their bickering ended prematurely, Kate and Carly exchange dirty looks before going their separate ways to class.

Sophie shakes her head, watching them go. "I don't know what gets into them sometimes." She turns back to me. "Look, don't worry about the church thing, okay?" She pats me soothingly on the shoulder. "I know last night was weird and all, but those people are harmless."

Yeah, whatever. Tell that to all the gays and other people who don't conform to those "harmless" people's religious ideals. I don't say that to Sophie, though, because I know she doesn't mean it like that. She's just one of those people who sees the best in everyone. "Okay," I agree, which is just as well since the first-period bell rings then, preventing further discussion on the topic.

I decide to put last night out of my mind and focus all my energy on my new goal: legal emancipation.

During study hall that afternoon, I manage to wrangle a pass to the computer lab, supposedly to work on a research paper for English, but in reality I intend to trawl the Internet for info about this amazing legal process that will hopefully free me from Sherri's clutches. But when I enter the drafty room, the only two computers are occupied by a couple of geeky-looking guys playing some computer game.

I hover behind them, leaning forward to make sure the scent of my perfume wafts over them. Ten seconds later they're tripping over each other on their way out of the lab.

Smiling, I settle myself in one of the chairs. They didn't both have to leave, but whatever. I pull up Google and type in "legal emancipation." I read for several minutes, my excitement growing as I read each requirement. "Legal source of income." Check. I have my trust fund. "Ability to manage own finances." Like that would be an issue—I've been using credit cards since I was nine. The last requirement, unfortunately, is a bit more problematic. "Parent/guardian approval." I reread the words, confused. WTH kind of a requirement is that? I mean, isn't the whole point of emancipation because you're NOT getting along with your parent/guardian? Meaning you're probably trying to do something they don't agree with (like live in L.A.). So why on earth would they approve of you being emancipated when you're just going to run off and do whatever it is they don't approve of?

I look for some sort of elaboration on this point, but my search turns up nothing. Which means it's time to call Luke. Glancing up to make sure the room monitor is still absorbed in the book she was reading when I came in, I slip my cell phone out of my purse and punch in the number. Yes, I know the phone number of my dad's attorney by heart. Sad, isn't it? But that's the way the past year has been.

"Collier, Rose, Hargrove, and Elliot," the receptionist says in her smooth, cultured voice. Everything about Collier, Rose is smooth and cultured, from the coolly beautiful receptionist to the elegant cream-and-white waiting area with the silver tea service. They're one of the most prestigious law firms in L.A., which is saying something since there are a lot of prestigious law firms in L.A. Except they didn't get Daddy off or keep Sherri from getting custody of me, so I'm not sure I'm all that impressed. But Daddy still thinks they're the best, so I'll give them the benefit of the doubt.

As always, Luke is in a meeting. He's ALWAYS in a meeting, the same as everyone else in L.A. God forbid somebody should actually take a call, lest it appear they're not totally swamped with work. I leave Luke a voice mail asking him to call me. After double-checking to make sure my phone is set on vibrate, I return to my Google research.

I'm scrolling through search results when somebody plops down at the computer next to me.

"Hey."

I glance over to see who has spoken and am shocked when I realize it's Jaci, the girl Sophie said was so mean to Kate when they were little.

"Hey." I turn back to my screen, hoping to discourage her from trying to engage in further interaction.

"I like your purse," she says, reaching out to touch the strap of my Louis V. "It's really cute."

I keep my gaze firmly fixed on the monitor. "Thanks."

"You're welcome." There's a long moment of silence, then she gives a delicate cough, clearly intended to get my attention.

I consider asking her what she wants, but then I check the time in the bottom corner of the computer screen. Only six minutes until I have to go back to study hall. I ignore her.

She coughs again, louder this time.

I continue ignoring her. Unless she coughs up a lung or some other internal organ, I have no intention of even glancing at her.

Finally, she blurts, "Kate White told me you made the top she has on."

Man, what is this chick's deal? I think, frustrated. "That's right," I reply still not looking at her. And then the lightbulb switches on, and I realize why she's here ruining my precious Internet time. I squeeze my eyes shut. Please don't say it, please don't say it, please don't—

"Could you make me something too?" she asks eagerly.

Damn. She said it. I open my eyes reluctantly and turn my head to tell her no way. Except now she's fumbling for something in her purse (a Prada knockoff—you can spot them a mile away), words pouring out of her mouth like some sort of verbal dam has burst inside her head. "See, like, there's this cheer competition in Dallas coming up, and on the last night, everybody goes out, you know? Like to a club? And all the other girls are from big cities, so they, like, have all these designer clothes from cool shops, you know? But we don't have anything like that, and last year a couple of girls made fun of me." She withdraws a magazine clipping and thrusts it toward me. "But I want this year to be different."

I take the clipping from her, mentally cursing myself for being such a wimp. Because now I feel just a teeny bit sorry for her. She may be the Queen Bee here, but outside Possum Grape, she's just a plain old worker bee. *Get a grip, West*, I tell myself sternly. *This is the girl who practically ruined Kate's life. She doesn't deserve your sympathy. Not to mention that Sophie would be furious if you agreed to help her.*

But then Maria's voice butts in, reminding me that everyone deserves a second chance. And then my Buddhist meditation teacher throws his two cents in by pointing out that helping Jaci would be good for my karma. You know, what goes around comes around and all that. I mean, just look at Jaci—she made fun of Kate when they were little, and now her fellow cheerleaders are making fun of her.

My internal war must be obvious because Jaci suddenly looks embarrassed. She snatches the clipping out of my hand and shoves it back in her purse. "Never mind," she mutters, not meeting my eyes. "Just forget I said anything, okay?" She gets up from her seat.

"No, wait." I put out my arm to stop her. "Sure, I can make something for you." OMG, did I actually just say that? Am I freaking insane?

"Really?" She looks back at me, her face brightening. "That would be so great."

"Yeah," I echo. "Great." Assuming Kate doesn't have me killed.

"So do I need to, like, do anything?" she asks. "Give you my measurements or something?"

"Um, yeah. Listen, can we talk about it later?" I jerk my chin toward the computer. "I'm kind of in the middle of something here."

"Yeah. Sure. Talk to you later." She gives me a little wave and leaves.

FINALLY. I heave a sigh of relief and turn back to the computer to see how much time I have left to finish searching for legal emancipation info. The answer is exactly none. Great, now I won't know anything else until I talk to Luke. Frustrated, I close the screen and head back to study hall to stare at my cell and wait for him to call.

Of course he calls during my class with the cell phone Nazi.

"You have three minutes. Go."

I hunch down in my seat, trying to look as if I'm resting my head against my hand instead of holding a cell phone to my ear. Not that I'm scared of the cell phone Nazi, but I don't necessarily care to provoke him either.

Still, I'm not about to tell Luke I can't talk. It could be days before he calls back, and I've got to get this emancipation thing rolling NOW. And it's not like I'm the only person ignoring Mrs. Lawson, or Mrs. La-La, as I've dubbed her since she's so spacey. Half the class is whispering and passing notes behind her back as she dreamily scrawls equations on the chalkboard, totally oblivious to everything except whatever titillating mathematical fantasy is going on in her head. I mean, the guy across from me is listening to his MP3 player, okay? That's how structured this class is.

"I want to get legally emancipated," I tell Luke in a low voice, barely over a whisper. It doesn't do any good. As soon as the words are out of my mouth, I feel a familiar rapping between my shoulder blades. I groan inwardly. Great. I flap my hand impatiently over my shoulder, signaling for him to lay off for a minute.

"Can't help you," Luke replies curtly. "Anything else?"

"Why can't you help me?" I'm annoyed at his abruptness, which is even worse than usual. I mean, it's not like this is pro bono or anything. He's totally going to charge my dad, like, three hundred dollars for this call.

"Because you're in another state. You'll have to hire a local attorney if you want to pursue emancipation. Anything else?"

I mentally picture him pushing back the sleeve of his Versace suit to check his TAG to see how much of my three minutes is left. Sometimes I think Daddy needs to find a less successful attorney, one who isn't quite so self-important.

"Why can't you—hey!" I whirl around as the psycho suddenly yanks the cell phone out of my hand.

He waves it above his head. "Mrs. Lawson! The new girl is using her cell phone during class." He says it like a little kid telling on a playmate—*Mommy! Susie took my shovel.*

Mrs. La-La startles at the sound of her name. She looks surprised when she turns away from the board and sees the class looking back at her, as if she forgot she was in the room with other people. "Who needs a cell phone?" she asks dazedly.

"He does," I say quickly, not about to squander the advantage of having a senile teacher. "He has to make an important call. To his doctor. It's really serious." I cup my hand around my mouth and say in a stage whisper, "Swollen testicle. But don't worry," I add in my normal voice, "I told him he could use my phone."

Several people titter. Psycho makes a strangled sound, but he seems to be having trouble forming actual words.

Likewise, Ms. La-La is also at a loss. "Oh, my. Yes, well. That is serious." She gazes fearfully around the class, as if worried more students are going to share embarrassing info about their genitalia.

Finally, the psycho starts to croak out something intelligible, but Mrs. La-La says hastily, "No, no, dear. We don't want to hear any more. That's a personal matter between you and your physician." She hurries toward the back of the room, her long skirt swishing. Stopping in front of psycho, she plucks my phone out of his hand and hands it back to me. "It was very sweet of West to let you use her phone, but health issues are something that should be dealt with outside of school." She pats him on the shoulder and swishes back to the chalkboard.

I can feel the psycho's murderous stare boring into my back. Judging from the amount of snickering and giggling going on, I doubt if anyone's going to let him forget this little incident any-time soon. Darn. And I was hoping he'd ask me to prom.

16
No Good Deed Goes Unpunished

As soon as we get to JoLynn's I ask Sophie for a phone book. "You don't need the yellow pages to find a lawyer," she says, laughing, when I tell her why I need it. "There's only one lawyer in town—Dub Boyette. His office is just down the street."

One lawyer, and his name is Dub. I immediately think of that nursery jingle: "Rub-a-dub-dub, three men in a tub." I'm going to ask for legal advice from a man I'm now picturing in a bathtub with two other men. Perfect.

Sophie unearths a phone book and looks up Dub's office number. I punch the numbers into my cell as she reads them aloud. On the third ring, a machine picks up and a prerecorded message informs me that the office is closed until next week due to turkey season. "You've got to be kidding me."

"About what?" Sophie asks, glancing up from the swing top she just began cutting out for Dakota.

"His office is closed for *turkey season*."

Before she can say anything to make me feel better, JoLynn appears in the doorway. "West, there's a girl out here looking for you," she informs me.

"For me?" I repeat, startled. Who in the world would come to JoLynn's looking for me?

"Who is it?" Sophie asks her mom at the exact same moment Jaci Burton materializes in the doorway next to JoLynn.

"Her," JoLynn replies curtly. She jerks her chin toward Jaci, then turns on her heel and leaves.

My stomach drops. *At least Kate isn't here,* I think gratefully.

Sophie stares at Jaci, obviously stunned. "What are you doing—?" she begins, but Jaci is already walking toward me, words pouring out of her mouth in a giant run-on sentence.

"Hey West I know you said we'd talk about measurements and stuff later but I need this done pretty fast and I've noticed how you've been hanging out with Sophie so I thought maybe there was a chance you were here at the store so I decided to stop by in case you were so you could go ahead and take my measurements 'cause like I said I need this done kind of fast." She stops abruptly to suck in a breath, then looks at me expectantly.

"Er—okay," I say awkwardly, acutely aware of Sophie's gaze, which is now burning a hole through my forehead.

"Great." Jaci heaves her knockoff Prada onto the table and offers me a dazzling smile.

"West, can I talk to you for a minute?" Sophie's voice is chillingly polite.

I snatch a soft measuring tape off the table. "Sure, uh, just let me take care of this first, okay?" I whip the tape around Jaci's waist, not even bothering to tell her to pull up her shirt so I can get the most accurate measurement. I have to get her out of here as quickly as possible so I can try to explain my temporary insanity to Sophie.

After doing an equally half-assed job on the rest of Jaci's measurements, I scribble the numbers on a piece of paper, thrust her faux Prada into her arms, and usher her to the door before Sophie can kill her. Or me. Or both of us. I'm pretty sure she was looking at a pair of pinking shears very strangely just now.

"I'll talk to you at school, okay?" I tell Jaci, pushing her out of the workroom.

"O-kay," Jaci replies, obviously annoyed at being thrown out. "You've got the clipping I gave you, right?"

I nod. "Absolutely," I say firmly, even though I have no idea where her clipping is.

The second I shut the door, Sophie explodes. "What do you think you're doing?" she cries incredulously. "I told you what Jaci did to Kate. I told you she was awful. Did you think I was kidding or something?" She stares at me with a mixture of shock and hurt, like I'm a pet that has suddenly turned on her.

"I know what you're thinking," I tell her, trying to explain. "But it's not what it looks like."

"What is it, then? Because it looks like you're making her a dress, West."

I collapse onto a chair. I have no idea how I'm going to make Sophie understand why I agreed to Jaci's request. What am I supposed to say? That the woman who raised me whispers things in my head, even though she's currently a gajillion miles away? "I understand why you're mad, Sophie. It's just that she caught me off guard when I was in the computer lab and I didn't know what to say and—"

"You should have said no," Sophie interjects. "The same way I did at lunch that day."

"I was going to!" I cry. "But then Maria started saying all this stuff about everybody deserving a second chance and not judging—" I break off because I know I'm not making any sense.

"Look, I don't care what Maria says. Jaci doesn't deserve anything." She picks up the pile of clothes we've been working on for Dakota and thrusts them at me. "Here. You can pay my mom for what you owe her on your way out."

"Sophie, please. Don't do this. I'll call Jaci and tell her I changed my mind." The hell with Maria and her second chances. Sophie is one of the few things keeping me sane in this place.

She shakes her head. "I'm sorry. Everything's different now. I can't trust you." She rushes out of the room before I can protest any further.

Defeated, I gather up my things. I can't bear the thought of facing JoLynn, so I simply write a check for five hundred dollars and leave it on the table. It's far more money than the actual cost of what I used, but I don't care.

I slip through the store as unobtrusively as possible. Sophie, thankfully, is nowhere to be found and JoLynn is helping a customer, so it's not very difficult. As I set off down the sidewalk it occurs to me that I have no way to get home now that I've ruined things with Sophie. I've been depending on her to take me home after school every day so I don't have to ride the school bus. Great. Now I'll have to call Sherri to come pick me up, which will no doubt lead to all sorts of awkward questions.

Wanting to avoid the inevitable for as long as possible, I wander along the sidewalk peering in the shop windows. As I'm peering into the window of the hardware store, my cell phone trills inside my purse. I dig it out and check the display, thinking maybe Sophie changed her mind. My face splits into a relieved grin the instant I see the familiar number. It's even better than Sophie. Delaney is FINALLY calling me back.

I rip open the phone. "OMG, where have you been?"

"Alice is gone." Delaney's voice is tremulous, as if she's trying not to cry.

Damn Alice, I think silently. She's obviously being a psychobitch again. "I'm sorry," I tell Delaney gently. "I know how hard it is when she's on the rampage."

"No, she's not gone as in freaking out," Delaney corrects me. "She's gone as in gone."

Uh-oh. Delaney has apparently dived into her emergency stash, because she's not making any sense. "Gone where?" I say, playing along. You can't argue with somebody under the influence. You just have to humor them.

"To New Jersey," she replies, sounding surprisingly lucid. "The dean of the psych department at Princeton asked her to fill in for some professor."

Wow. She must be doing something more serious than pot. "Have you been with Rachel?" I ask, referring to our circle's resident drug queen. You know, the girl who went to rehab instead of camp when we were, like, ten. "What did she give you?" It would be just like Rachel to take advantage of Delaney when she's vulnerable.

"West, I'm being totally serious. My dad just took Alice to LAX. She's going to be gone for four months."

I frown. Delaney really DOES sound pretty with it, but there's no way what she's saying is true. Crazy-evil people like Alice don't just conveniently leave for four months. You have to drive a stake through their heart or shoot them with a silver bullet to get rid of them.

"May Jude Law go bald and get a potbelly if I'm not telling the truth," Delaney adds.

OMG. She really is telling the truth, I realize, dumbfounded. She would never jeopardize Jude unless she was totally serious.

"Alice is gone. To New Jersey. For four months," I repeat slowly, savoring each word. For a moment, neither of us says anything, but then we both erupt into high-pitched squeals.

"So when will you be back?" Delaney asks breathlessly after we finish screaming with joy. "Our party is in a week."

My joy dampens a little. "Soon," I answer vaguely.

"Did you pay off your aunt?"

"Uh, no. That didn't exactly work out. But it's okay," I add quickly, thinking about Brooke Davenport and legal emancipation. "I've got another plan."

17

Revenge Is a Dish Best Served in Ugly Plaid

"I said HEY!"

At the sound of the loud voice, I startle guiltily and jerk my forehead away from the cool metal of my locker.

Jaci is standing next to me. "What are you doing?" she asks, frowning at me.

"Er, nothing."

"Were you *sleeping*?"

"No. I was just, um, thinking about something." Actually, I really WAS sleeping. Even though most of it is only half finished, Dakota was so excited over the clothes Sophie and I made for her, she decided to show her gratitude by sleeping in the bottom bunk with me. Apparently to a six-year-old, sticking your foot in someone's face while they're trying to sleep is the same as sending a thank-you card. Still, I'm not about to admit to Jaci that I was napping against my locker.

She seems to accept this. "I just wanted to make sure we were on the same page about the dress."

I sigh wearily. I've decided to tell her I've changed my mind. "Look, Jaci, I don't think—" I break off as Steven suddenly passes by my locker and winks suggestively at me. The whole incident is only a split second, but it totally catches me off guard. I stare at his muscled back as he continues down the hall.

Jaci is staring too. "Yummy, isn't he?" she murmurs.

"Mmmmm," I agree, Steven's sudden appearance apparently rendering me incapable of forming actual words.

"He's good in bed, too," she adds.

My ability to speak returns instantaneously. "What?" I say, swiveling my head to gape at her.

"Sometimes good-looking guys aren't, you know," she continues, twirling her finger around one of her hair extensions.

"You and Steven used to go out?"

"God, no." She laughs. "I just slummed with him for a little while. My daddy would tan my hide if I went out with a guy like Steven Kinney."

"Why? What's wrong with Steven?"

She slaps me playfully on the shoulder. "Don't act stupid. You know what I'm talking about."

"No, I really *don't* know what you're talking about. Why wouldn't your dad want you to date him?"

Now she looks annoyed. "Duh—maybe because he's poor and he's not white?" she says impatiently.

BITCH! It's all I can do not to say the word out loud.

Sophie was right: Jaci hasn't changed at all. It was crazy of me to give her the benefit of the doubt.

"So, anyway," Jaci continues, Steven already forgotten, "I just wanted to double-check one more time to make sure that you have the clipping and that you know what to do."

I open my mouth to tell her that she and her clipping can go to hell, but then it occurs to me that maybe there's another, more gratifying way to let Jaci know what I think of her. "Don't worry," I say, giving her a saccharine-laced smile. "I know *exactly* what to do."

The morning goes by torturously slow, partly because, well, it's the morning and partly because I'm impatient to talk to Sophie. I know she's pissed at me, but once she hears what I'm going to do to Jaci, she'll totally get over it. At least I hope she'll get over it. She was pretty mad. And now Emmylou, Carly, and Kate probably know, so I'm sure they're mad too.

The instant the bell rings for lunch, I rush to the cafeteria. I brace myself as I approach the table, expecting everyone to give me the cold shoulder, but to my surprise, everyone acts totally normal.

Carly waves a stalk of broccoli at me. "We were wondering if you were coming."

I steal a glance at Sophie, who is pointedly trying to avoid looking at me. She didn't tell them, I realize, surprised.

"Are you going to stand up the whole lunch period or what?" Kate asks, peering at me with—well, I wouldn't classify the expression in her eyes as *fondness*, but it's definitely not hate, either.

"Actually, I need to talk to Sophie privately for a few minutes." Now that I know Sophie didn't tell them, I'm not about to ruin things by talking in front of them.

Predictably, this announcement startles everyone, since a request to talk "privately" usually means you want to rip apart the people from whom you've just escaped. "What are you doing?" Sophie hisses, finally turning in her chair to look at me.

"Please. Just for a minute," I plead, doing my best to look pitiful.

"What's going on?" Carly asks loudly.

"Nothing," Sophie replies, getting up abruptly from her chair. "We'll be right back." As soon as we're out of earshot, she whirls around to face me. "I told you—"

"You were right about Jaci," I interrupt. "She hasn't changed."

"Thanks for the news flash," Sophie says sarcastically. She turns to leave, but I grab her arm.

"Sophie, wait. I have a plan. I—"

"Congratulations," she cuts me off. She shrugs off my hand and turns to leave again.

Man. Who would have thought sweet, angel-faced Sophie was hiding such a temper? No wonder Emmylou and Carly cow down to her. "I'm going to make Jaci a hideous outfit so she'll look like a moron on her trip," I blurt as she's walking away.

She freezes midstride, then slowly turns back to face me. "What did you say?"

"I'm going to make Jaci a hideous outfit," I repeat. "And then I'm going to convince her to wear it to her cheerleading thingy."

"How hideous?" Sophie asks suspiciously.

"So hideous, Björk wouldn't even be caught dead in it. I'm going to make Jaci look like a complete idiot."

For a second, Sophie looks hesitant, but then her face splits into a grin and she throws her arms around me the way she did that first day in the bathroom when I gave her the stain-remover cloth. "Not without me, you're not."

"Type in 'worst-dressed celebrities,'" I instruct Sophie as she pulls up Google on JoLynn's laptop. It's after school, and we're crammed into JoLynn's tiny office at the back of the store. We've decided to do a little research before we embark on PHJ (Project Humiliate Jaci), and, unlike Sherri, JoLynn is actually a full-fledged member of the twenty-first century, possessing both a computer AND Internet access.

"Nine hundred and forty-three thousand results," Sophie reads from the screen.

"Just click on one," I tell her, waving my hand at the screen.

Obediently, she moves the cursor. "'Mr. Blackwell's best- and worst-dressed celebrity list,'" she reads aloud, which is totally unnecessary since I'm looking at the screen over her shoulder. "Britney Spears, Mary-Kate Olsen, Jessica Simpson—" Sophie breaks off. "Hey, what's wrong with Jessica Simpson?" she asks the picture of Mr. Blackwell. "I like the way she dresses." She sticks her tongue out at the picture and continues reading. "Eva Longoria, Mariah Carey, Paris Hilton, Anna Nicole Smith, Shakira, Lindsay Lohan—*Lindsay Lohan*?" She glances up at me. "What's wrong with this dude?"

"He's just old. This isn't what we need, anyway," I say impatiently. "We need pictures of what made them the worst-dressed, not just the list." Even though I already have an idea in mind for Jaci's "dress," I don't want to leave any tacky stone unturned. "Ooooh, I know." I jostle Sophie's shoulder as I have a sudden brain wave. "Just put in Juliette Lewis."

"Good idea," Sophie compliments me.

Fifteen minutes later, we've printed a whole slew of photos from which to draw inspiration. Juliette's a cool actress, but her clothing ensembles are enough to render even the most acid-tongued style critic speechless. Although it pains me to admit it, we also come up with a couple of pics of Sarah Jessica Parker and Gwyneth Paltrow—SJP in that super-scary tartan-plaid thing she wore to the Met's Costume Institute Gala a couple of years ago, and Gwynnie in the now-infamous goth dress from the 2002 Oscars. You know—the one that made her breasts look like they sagged down to her waist? Which just proves that even the most stylish women in the world can screw up occasionally.

We take the pictures back to the workroom to study them and talk about our options, but just as we're fanning them out on the table, the door bangs open and a distressed-looking JoLynn rushes in with a poufy wedding gown cradled over her arms. "We have an emergency," she tells Sophie breathlessly, coming to a halt in front of us.

Sophie looks concerned. "What's wrong, Mama?"

"Beth Ann Whitfield's wedding is this weekend, and her dress is too small. She can't get it zipped."

Sophie frowns. "But I thought you made her wedding dress. Did she decide to order one or something?"

JoLynn shakes her head. "No, I made it. Apparently Beth Ann has been using Oreo milkshakes to calm her pre-wedding jitters."

Sophie and I snicker.

"Anyway," JoLynn continues, ignoring us even though she looks like she's about to laugh too, "it's going to be time consuming to let this out because of all the beading, so you're going to have to make the Possum Queen shirts, Sophie. Okay?"

Sophie nods obediently. "Okay."

"It doesn't have to be anything elaborate," JoLynn adds. "Just do something simple."

"Okay," Sophie repeats, her attention already focused back on the table. "I got it."

As soon as JoLynn leaves, I ask Sophie the obvious question. "Um, what exactly is a Possum Queen?"

"The person who wins the Possum Queen Pageant," she says absently, pulling a picture of Juliette toward her so she can study it more closely. "You know—at the end of the Possum Festival."

I sigh. This is annoyingly reminiscent of when I discovered Steven in the bathroom. "O-kay. What the hell is a Possum Festival?"

She glances up from the picture. "A party to celebrate Possum Day," she replies calmly, as if throwing a party in celebration of a rodent is totally normal, like shooting off fireworks on the Fourth of July. "It's next Saturday. Hey, do you want to go?" she asks, her expression suddenly becoming excited.

"Um, no."

"Oh, come on," she cajoles. "There'll be a band and barbecue and everything. And you'd have a really good shot at winning the Possum Queen Pageant," she adds. "They like blondes. Do you want me to sign you up? I think Mama has some forms up by the register."

The REALLY scary thing about this conversation is that she's totally serious. "I think I'll hold out for Badger Queen," I say dryly. "Besides, the party I was telling you about is next weekend." I don't add that I currently have no idea how I'm actually going to GET to the party.

"Oh." She looks disappointed. "Well, do you want to help me with the shirts?"

"Sure," I say, relieved she's not going to press the issue. "What do you have to do exactly?" Helping with a few shirts is a small price to pay for not having to vie for the title of Possum Queen.

She waves her hand dismissively. "Oh, it's no big deal. The Possum Pageant Board gives all the contestants a T-shirt that says 'Possum Queen' and the year on it. You know, as a memento. Mama's already got the T-shirts. She usually just uses her embroidery machine for the words."

I nod. "Okay. We can work on the shirts and Jaci's outfit at the same time."

I've just started perusing the pictures again, when a thought suddenly occurs to me. I lift up my head and poke Sophie in the arm. "Hey. Why don't *you* compete in the pageant? You're blond."

She throws her head back and laughs.

"I knew it!" I say triumphantly. "It's not really a pageant—it's some kind of embarrassing thing, isn't it? And you were trying to get me to be in it!" I have a vague image of the locals convincing unsuspecting suckers like me to get up on a stage and put, like, hats made out of possum fur on their heads.

"Oh no, it's a real pageant," Sophie says, shaking her head.

I narrow my eyes. "Then why don't you sign up for it?"

She makes a show of pretending to fluff her hair. "I can't," she says airily. "I was Miss Possum Queen 2005."

18

Chiggers

On Saturday morning I wake up to discover that I've slept until SEVEN a.m., one whole hour longer than normal. I immediately jolt out of bed to check the top bunk, already feeling tearful since Dakota is obviously either dead or close to dead. Because I'm pretty sure that's the only thing that could keep her from waking me up at dawn, with the possible exception of if she was kidnapped during the night. But even then she'd probably insist that her abductor bring her back by six a.m. so she could jump on my head.

When I stand on my tiptoes to look, however, the top bunk is totally empty. I drop back down on my heels. OMG. Somebody really DID kidnap her.

I fly out of the room and race to the kitchen, trying to remember if Daddy has any friends in law enforcement. There was that one guy he used to play tennis with who was in the FBI. Or was it the CIA? Or was it the—

"West, look, I'm cooking!"

I careen to a halt, banging my hip against the corner of the kitchen table. The entire family is in the kitchen—including Dakota, who is standing on a chair that's pushed up in front of the stove, beaming at me.

"See?" she says proudly, waving the plastic spatula in her hand. As if to prove her point, she takes the spatula and pushes it around inside the frying pan in front of her.

Sherri is by the stove too, overseeing Dakota's movements. "Good job," she says approvingly. "Don't forget to flip that last piece of bacon."

I pull out a chair from the table and plop down in it, relieved. Dakota isn't the victim of a kidnapping; she's just busy learning how to cook bacon so she'll be able to properly clog her own husband's and children's arteries someday.

Clint flicks his gaze up from his Game Boy for half a second, "Hey."

"Hey," I reply, even though he's already absorbed in the screen again. Exchanging monosyllabic words are about as impressive as our interactions get, but at least he doesn't hate me anymore. I'm SO glad he finally got over the truck thing.

When it comes to Joe, on the other hand, swapping one-syllable words would be an improvement. I've pretty much given up on attempting to talk to him altogether since the only response I ever get is a grunt. He's like that with everybody, though, so I'm not taking it personally or anything. He's just a man of few words. And many grunts.

I'm amusing myself with the headlines on the cover of the magazine he's reading ("Blaster Removes Potato Bugs without Chemicals!" "Low-Cost Tractor Forks!") when Sherri suddenly calls out from the stove, "Oh West, hon, the weatherman said the pollen count is low right now, so this would be a good day for you to take care of those weeds by the mailbox."

What? Is she kidding me? The pollen thing was supposed to be, like, a foolproof plan. I try to play it cool. "I really wish I could, Aunt Sherri, but I promised Sophie I'd spend the day helping her make T-shirts for the Possum Queen Pageant." Which is actually not even a lie. Sophie is supposed to pick me up at eleven so we can go back to the store and finish working on Jaci's outfit and the Possum Queen shirts.

Sherri smiles reassuringly. "Don't worry. Those weeds will only take a jiffy, hon. You'll still have plenty of time left to help Sophie."

A jiffy. Great. I feel so much better.

"Clinty will show you how to use the weedeater before we leave," she adds.

"You're leaving?" I reply automatically. Ooops. I didn't mean to sound quite so eager.

Sherri nods. "We're going up to Toad Suck to see about a bull," she informs me before turning back to the bacon.

Toad Suck, of course. I guess there were no bulls available in Fly Vomit or Rat Entrails.

Have I mentioned that I can't wait to get out of here?

One hour later, I'm prematurely aging under the hot sun and fighting with a piece of lawn-care machinery designed by a sadist. Although Sherri referred to it as a "weedeater," the stupid thing hasn't eaten so much as a blade of grass so far. Of course, maybe if Clint had done something helpful like actually shown me how to operate it instead of just handed it to me as he left, I might have some sort of clue about what I'm doing.

Hmmph. Maybe he's not totally over the truck thing, after all.

Swatting away one of the numerous mosquitoes that keep trying to give me West Nile, I aim the machine at the tangled mess of weeds yet again. *Please work*, I beg silently. After almost a full minute, I step back.

The evil plants look exactly the same.

"Aaaargh!" I throw down the worthless machine and drop onto my knees. Fine. I'll just pull the stupid things up with my bare hands. Okay, my gardening-glove-clad hands.

I grab viciously at the weeds, cursing under my breath with each yank. In fact, I work myself up into such a lather that I don't even notice the giant black snake until he slithers past my knees. As in he *touches* my knees. Let me say that all together: A GIANT SNAKE TOUCHES ME.

Reflexively, I open my mouth to scream, but the only sound that comes out is a hoarse little squeak. Shutting it, I glance around frantically, looking for something I can use to defend myself. There's a palm-size rock that looks pretty heavy about a foot away from my left hand, but I'm too scared to actually move to reach for it. And assuming I DO manage to grab it somehow, then what will I do—ask him if he can identify it as shale, quartz, or limestone? Because I'm pretty sure I'm not brave enough to do anything like throw it at him.

Out of my peripheral vision, I catch sight of his black body as he glides out onto the gravel road. While I'm practically paralyzed with fear, he looks totally unconcerned; he's just out taking his morning slither, scaring the crap out of any humans he happens to run into. He's probably laughing at me right now, the bastard. *I really SHOULD get that rock and throw it at him,* I think meanly. Except I'm not that stupid. And for anyone who thinks I'm acting like a wuss, I have four words for you: *Snakes on a Plane.* Rent it and then we'll talk.

After what seems like an eternity, he FINALLY meanders his way across the road and disappears into the tall grass on the opposite side. The instant his body is out of sight, I stagger to my feet and run for my life.

I'm so upset by the time I get back to the house that I don't even attempt to calm myself down. I just go straight to the emergency stash of Xanax in my suitcase, even though I know that taking even one of the little white pills will put me right to sleep and Sophie will be here in less than two hours. Arielle would be mortified if she knew I was using a pharmaceutical "crutch" to help get my emotions under control, but I don't care. There are some things positive thinking just can't fix, and being touched by a giant snake is one of them.

I wake up because I'm on fire. I jerk up in the bunk bed, batting at my legs and stomach, but then I realize I'm not actually on fire—my skin just itches so fiercely, I feel like I am. Panicked, I throw off the covers and run down the hall to the bathroom.

By the time I get there, I've moved beyond feeling like I'm on fire to a torturous sensation I can't even describe. Frantic, I rip off my clothes. And almost pass out because my body is COVERED in angry red lesions.

I yank down the bath towel that's hanging over the shower curtain rod and whip it around my body before flinging open the door to run back to the bedroom for my cell phone so I can call 911 or the Centers for Disease Control or whomever you call when you suddenly develop leprosy. Except I can't go anywhere because Steven is standing in the doorway.

I'm not even surprised to see him. I mean, who else would I run into while covered in skin lesions and wearing a towel? It's practically a given at this point.

"Move," I order, trying to push past him.

He doesn't budge. "What's wrong?"

I shove roughly against his chest. "I'm dying, okay? Now move."

"Not until you tell me what's wrong."

"I just told you what's wrong!" I say furiously. "I'm dying." I shove his chest even harder, but it's like trying to move a brick wall.

"*Why* do you think you're dying?"

Instead of trying to explain, I hold out my right leg so he can see the proof for himself. I watch his face closely as he examines the bites on my calf, waiting for him to recoil in disgust or run for a phone himself, but instead, he starts to LAUGH. Not a little snicker or even a chuckle, but a full-out belly laugh.

"What are you laughing at?" I demand, dropping my leg. "Can't you see I have a serious condition?" I push him again, even though I know it's futile. "Get out of my way. I have to get to a hospital."

He braces his arms across the doorway so I can't escape. "You don't have to go to the hospital. You're fine. You just got into some chiggers."

"What are chiggers?" I ask suspiciously.

"Microscopic bugs that burrow into your skin."

"Bugs?" I repeat shrilly. "I have *bugs* under my skin?"

"Well, technically they're not really *under* your skin," he replies calmly. "They just sort of suck up your skin cells with this little straw thing."

This last bit of info is what sends me over the edge. "Get them off me!" I scream, hysterically slapping at my legs.

"It's all right," Steven says loudly, grabbing my hands so I can't hit myself anymore. I struggle against him, wishing I could rip my skin off. I'm not a wimp, but the idea of bugs sucking on my skin like it's a smoothie or something is just too much, especially on the heels of the snake incident.

He steers me back into the bathroom. "You just need to take a bath in some bleach water," he says soothingly. He pushes me into a sitting position on the closed toilet lid and turns on the bathtub. "Stay here," he tells me, once he's adjusted the water to a satisfactory temperature. He leaves, reappearing a few moments later with a jug of bleach. He pours some into the tub and swishes it around.

I don't even protest when he tells me to get in, even though submerging your skin in bleach is almost as bad as standing out in the sun without sunscreen.

"Just soak in there for a while," he orders. "There's calamine lotion on the counter. Put it on when you get out."

I soak in the bleach for as long as I can stand it. I itch EVERYWHERE now. Even my scalp itches, but I'm too scared to dip my head in the water, in case the bleach might make my hair fall out or something. When I finally can't take the fumes any longer, I dry myself off and rub on the lotion, which basically turns my whole body pink. And not only does it make me look like I bathed in Pepto-Bismol instead of bleach, it doesn't do jack for the itching. I want to scrub my skin with a wire brush.

A folded T-shirt is lying on the counter, also apparently left by Steven, so I pull it over my head.

When I finally emerge from the bathroom, he's waiting for me in the hall. "Are you okay?"

I open my mouth intending to tell him everything is fine, but to my complete shock, I burst into tears. And not delicate, ladylike tears, but huge, racking sobs that shake my whole body. All of a sudden I feel overwhelmed by everything. My dad, Sherri, being here—it's all just too much.

Steven wraps his arms around me and pulls me down to the ground with him so that I'm sitting in his lap. And then he just lets me cry it out. He doesn't shush me or try to insist that everything will be fine; he just rocks me back and forth and strokes my hair. I don't know how long I cry, but by the time I finish, I'm totally exhausted.

"Better?" Steven asks softly.

I lift my head out of the crook of his shoulder, which is drenched. "No. My back itches like hell."

He laughs and starts gently rubbing my back through the T-shirt. "It's better not to scratch, you know. It'll take them longer to heal."

I close my eyes, reveling in the temporary relief. "I don't care. I can't stand it."

"So are you going to tell me what that was all about?" he asks after a few moments, still rubbing my back.

"No," I reply, not opening my eyes.

His hand immediately disappears from my back. "Are you sure you don't want to tell me?" he says teasingly, wiggling his fingers at me. "Because if you don't, I think my fingers are getting pretty tired."

I thrust out my lower lip. "That's just cruel. You're taking advantage of my weakened condition." Speaking of my weakened condition, it suddenly occurs to me that it's probably not a good idea to be sitting on his lap like this. Because he's still REALLY hot. And I'm not thinking very clearly right now. And we all know what happened the last time I was in close proximity to him when I wasn't thinking clearly.

I scramble off his lap and quickly sit on the floor beside him.

"I prefer to call it persuading you with charm," he grins.

For a moment I consider refusing just on principle, but

truthfully, I'm dying to tell someone about Zane and my problems. Plus, I ITCH. "Just remember that you asked for this," I warn. "And you have to scratch until I tell you to stop," I add.

He wiggles his fingers again. "Whatever you say."

It takes me almost forty-five minutes to tell him everything and by the time I'm finished he looks TOTALLY confused.

"So let me get this straight," he says, furrowing his brow. "You're trying to get some guy to sleep with you by making him a bunch of clothes?"

I roll my eyes. I KNEW he wouldn't understand. I mean, I'm not saying that he's dense or anything. It's just that feminine wiles are way beyond the comprehension of most guys. "I'm trying to get him to give me a *job* by making a bunch of clothes. If I did happen to sleep with him, that's just extra."

"So you're, like, going to try to sleep your way to the top of his company or something?"

"No!" I take a breath and go over it again, but when I finish, he only looks marginally less confused.

"You still don't understand, do you?"

"Yes, I do," he protests.

"Really?" I say, surprised. "So you get it?"

"Absolutely." He gets to his feet and grins down at me. "You're totally crazy."

"No, I'm n—"

"Hello? Is anyone home? West?"

My protest is interrupted by the sound of Sophie's voice coming from the front part of the house. Crap. In between discovering I'm now a mutant and pouring out my heart to Steven, I forgot all about her coming to pick me up. I didn't even hear her knock.

"I'm here, Soph," I call out. Flustered, I struggle to my feet. "I'll be out in a minute," I add, praying she stays where she is. The last thing I need is for her to see me alone in the hall with Steven, wearing nothing but a T-shirt. *His* T-shirt.

"I have to go," I tell him.

"So I gathered," he replies, still watching me with that amused expression.

"Thank you for helping me," I say sincerely.

He nods. "No problem. Anytime you want a bleach bath, I'm your guy."

I was actually referring more to him letting me cry on his shoulder (literally), but I leave it at that. There's no reason to get mushy about it or anything.

"How long before these things are gone, anyway?" I ask, bending down to claw—I mean scratch—my ankles.

I expect him to tell me a few days, or—worst-case scenario—an entire week. Instead, he answers, "Two or three weeks, give or take."

Perfect. I'll be the only person at the party with leprosy.

19

Dub's a Dud, but Jaci Is a Fashion Nightmare

"*That* is the ugliest thing I've ever seen in my life." It's after school on Monday, and Sophie and I have just unveiled what we have deemed our "Masterpiece" for Kate, who looks totally repulsed.

"It is, isn't it?" Sophie beams at the creation on the table like a proud mother gazing at her newborn.

"Seriously, you're not, like, going to wear that or anything, are you?" Kate persists. "Because that would definitely not be a good idea."

"It's for Jaci," I explain.

"Oh." Kate glances back down at the table. "Then never mind. It's perfect."

I nod because she's right. After the traumatic events of Saturday morning, when Sherri got back from Toad Kiss or wherever it is she went, I convinced her to let me spend the night with Sophie, and we spent the entire weekend holed up here, in JoLynn's backroom, laughing evilly like a couple of mad scientists and working our tails off (and, in my case, scratching my tail off). We didn't create a monster, but the dress we came up with is almost as scary.

Assuming she goes along with the plan Sophie and I have concocted, Jaci will dazzle the Dallas club scene in a one-piece tartan minidress held together on the sides with giant brass safety pins (sorry, Liz Hurley, you forgive me — right, darling?) and trimmed in bright red fur (faux, of course), topped off by a bustle of rainbow-colored ribbons.

"But do you think she'll really go for it?" Sophie pulls her hand away from the material, her expression suddenly doubtful.

"Yeah," Kate puts in. "Jaci's a bitch, but she's not stupid."

I give the bustle a little fluff before bending down to scratch my ankles. "Trust me."

When Jaci arrives five minutes later, I'm relieved to see that she's without her two blond friends in tow. Until I have her firmly convinced that I'm outfitting her in the hottest thing since J-Lo's infamous green Versace, the less interference the better.

"Where is it?" Jaci asks eagerly. She looks around the room as if hoping the dress will hear her and pop out on its own accord.

I quickly move in front of her to block her view of the table. "Actually, for a high-concept outfit like this, it's better to see it on first," I explain smoothly. "To get the full effect. Why don't you get undressed and we'll put it on you? Then you can look in the full-length mirror."

A lot of girls would probably balk at the suggestion of stripping down in front of three other girls and letting them dress her, but Jaci strips off her jeans and T-shirt without even batting an eyelash.

"Okay, close your eyes," I instruct her as I motion for Sophie to bring the dress. It takes us several minutes to get it on her because the safety pins keep popping off, and by the time we finally manage it, Kate is shaking so hard with silent laughter, she looks like she's having a seizure. "Stop it," I mouth, frowning at her. Even though Jaci looks totally ridiculous, we have to keep our cool for this to work.

I guide Jaci over to the mirror. "You can open your eyes now." Obediently, her lids flutter open. Her eyes widen at the first glimpse of her reflection, almost as if she doesn't recognize herself, but then her expression becomes unreadable.

Now is the time for me to kick in the Deschanel charm. "Isn't it fabulous?" I prompt, taking a step back as if to get a better look. "Those other girls are going to *die* with envy when they see you." I ignore Kate's sudden coughing fit and lean back in, lowering my voice as if I'm about to impart a highly classified State secret. "This is strictly hush-hush, but Jessica Simpson is wearing this exact same thing—except in red—to the MTV Video Awards."

The mention of J. S. finally gets a reaction out of her. "You design for Jessica Simpson?"

I nod. "All the time." Even though this is a huge, gigantic lie, I don't feel even a teeny-tiny bit guilty because this is one of those instances where the end TOTALLY justifies the means.

I thicken my *National Enquirer* plot. "She and Lindsay had a big fight over it, but—and this is just between you and me—Lindsay can be kind of a you-know-what, so I let Jessica have it."

"Lindsay *Lohan*?" She turns and gapes at me, the dress and her reflection totally forgotten.

"You look really great, Jaci." Sophie's soft-spoken compliment elicits another coughing fit from Kate, who, at this point, Jaci probably thinks has tuberculosis or something. I shoot Kate a warning look over my shoulder. I've almost gotten this wrapped up and I don't need her to blow it for me.

Jaci returns her attention to the mirror. "I do look really great," she says slowly. "It's very—" She turns to me. "What did you call it again?"

"High concept," I supply.

"Yes. High concept." She nods thoughtfully as if committing the term to memory and resumes admiring her reflection.

Sophie and I exchange looks, high-fiving each other with our eyes. Move over, Juliette Lewis. Jaci Burton is in the house.

As soon as Jaci leaves with her "high-concept" dress, I rush down the street toward Dub Boyette's office. Today is Monday, so according to his answering machine, he should be back from murdering innocent turkeys. Except it turns out I shouldn't have been so eager to see him because he nixes my plans for legal emancipation before I've even finished drinking the lukewarm coffee his secretary gave me.

At least I *think* it's coffee. It's been so long since I've had any, I could be mistaken.

"Convincing Judge Emory you'd be better off on your own instead of with Sherri Reynolds would be about as easy as herding cats," Dub informs me when I finish my sob story. The rickety ceiling fan circles lazily over his head, ruffling the thousand or so papers stacked haphazardly on his desk. At least I assume there's a desk somewhere under there. Between the papers and the empty Styrofoam cups and crumpled McDonald's bags, it's hard to tell. "But I WOULD be better off on my own," I argue, trying hard not to think about Luke's immaculate mahogany desk. Untidiness doesn't necessarily equal incompetence, right? And his outer office is actually quite attractive. Well, except for the frogs. Ceramic, stuffed, plastic—there are all kinds of the little amphibians out there. Apparently his secretary has a thing.

Dub shakes his head. "Judge Emory and the Reynoldses belong to the same church. He's been the men's Sunday school teacher there for years." He says this last part as if it's the definitive statement on the matter. As if I'm going to say, "Oh, pardon *me*. I didn't realize he was a *Sunday school teacher*. That changes EVERYTHING."

I frown at him. "What difference does that make?"

"A big one, if you're trying to prove Sherri Reynolds is an unfit guardian. He'd never believe it."

"It's not that she's *unfit*." I scratch my legs absently as I try to think of the easiest way to explain why I can't live with Sherri without going into my whole life story. "I mean, she's not, like, hitting me or chaining me up in the basement or anything. She's an okay person. It's just that I'd be better off on my own. You know—my best interest," I add, remembering the phrase that kept cropping up on Internet.

His Southern drawl is gentle, but firm. "I'm sorry, darling. There's just no way."

I stare at him dumbly, unable to believe what I'm hearing. He CAN'T be telling me there's no chance. "But what about separation of church and state?" I press, seizing the first semilucid thing that pops into my mind. "I thought judges were supposed to be impartial."

"Judges are only human, Miz Deschanel." His tone is less mild now, as if he's losing patience with me. "They're influenced by outside forces, just like the rest of us." He pauses for a moment before adding more kindly, "What's so bad about living with your aunt, anyway?"

"What's so bad about living with my aunt?" I repeat incredulously. "Let's see—so far, I've been mauled by dogs, attacked by a rooster, almost bitten by a cobra, and had bugs suck my skin with a straw." I sit the half-full coffee cup down on his desk with enough force to make part of the liquid slosh over the rim onto his desk. "*And* I sleep in a bunk bed." I sling my purse over my shoulder and get to my feet. "But clearly none of that matters to anyone, so I'll be on my way. Thanks for your time."

He shoots out of his chair, and for a second my spirits lift because I think he's going to stop me, but instead of shouting, "Wait! I had no idea things were that bad. I'll FORCE the judge to emancipate you!" he merely rounds the desk and hurries over to hold the door.

My heart sinks. I mistook his proper Southern manners for something that might actually help me.

"You sure do look like your mama," he comments as he ushers me into the outer office. The secretary looks up eagerly, straining to see us over the trio of stuffed frogs perched on the top of her computer monitor. I give her a wan smile. I don't resent her for being nosy. It's not her fault she lives in a town that's so boring, she has to amuse herself with ceramic frogs.

"Shame, her passing on that way," Dub continues, leading me to the front door. The bells tingle as he pulls it open. "She was a real sweet girl."

"Thanks," I say tiredly. Why is he talking about my mom? Does he really think that's, like, a pressing issue to me right now?

"Now, you be sure and give me a call if there's anything else I can help you with, you hear?" he orders as I stumble out into the bright afternoon sunlight.

Right. Because you were so much help this time.

I immediately call Delaney and tell her the bad news.

"But the party is Saturday," she wails. "What are you going to do?"

"I don't know," I tell her honestly. I SO cannot believe this is happening to me. I was so sure I'd be able to get emancipated and go on with my life. In L.A.

"Tristan has already been here setting things up," Delaney continues. "You know they're filming this for his special on the

Style network. He'll freak if your fashion show doesn't happen. He's planned everything around it."

Great. Way to make me feel even worse, Delaney. "I know. I'll think of something."

"Why don't you just ask your aunt if you can come back for the party?" she suggests. "You know—just for the weekend."

"But what good would that do?" I say miserably. "I still don't want to live here until I'm eighteen."

"I know," she says sympathetically. "But at least it would take care of the immediate crisis. And then you can figure the custody thing out later. I'm sure you guys will be able to come to some sort of agreement."

There she goes with that optimism thing again. Why can't she be normal and see the glass half empty like everybody else?

"Just ask her," Delaney urges.

I sigh. It's not exactly like I have a lot of other choices at the moment. "All right."

The more I think about Delaney's suggestion, the more it seems like a good idea, but before I get the chance to bring it up, Sherri drops a bombshell.

"Which do you prefer, hon, the tank or the river?" she asks me that night at dinner as I'm pretending to eat a fried chicken leg.

I freeze with the chicken leg suspended in front of my mouth. "What?"

"Tank or river," she repeats impatiently, as if I'm deliberately being obtuse.

"I have no idea what you're talking about."

She frowns. "I'm talking about your baptism, hon. Reverend Billy needs to know whether you want to be baptized in the tank at church or outside in the river so he can get things ready."

Whoa. My baptism? I put my chicken leg down on my plate, feeling as if somebody just darted out of nowhere and knocked me off balance.

Dakota claps her hands together. "Ooooh, do it in the river so the fishies can watch."

"I've already been baptized," I tell Sherri, hoping to nip this in the bud. "Maria's priest baptized me when I was little."

Sherri almost chokes on her chicken. "Her *priest*?" she says in a strangled voice. She gapes at me as if I've just admitted to being baptized by Marilyn Manson. "A *Catholic* priest?"

The others look equally appalled, even Dakota. Uh-oh. Apparently my Catholic baptism is a personal tidbit I should have kept to myself. "Er—I'm not really sure what he was," I lie.

"It's all right," Sherri says hoarsely, recovering her composure. She pats my hand reassuringly. "You were just a child. Everything will be fine after Reverend Billy baptizes you this Sunday."

This Sunday! But that's impossible, I moan silently. The party is Saturday night; I'll never be back in time. "Actually," I say hoarsely, "I need to talk to you about this weekend." She nods expectantly, so I continue. "There's this really important event in L.A. this Saturday that I need to fly back for. It's for charity," I add earnestly as Sherri starts shaking her head. Yeah, that's a total lie, but whatever.

"I'm sorry, hon. Your baptism is extremely important." She wrinkles her nose. "And I don't really think you have any business going back to that place."

Right. I have no business there. My house, my friends, my school, my father, Maria—they're all just totally inconsequential.

"Besides"—she smiles, taking a sip of her iced tea—"the Possum Queen Pageant is this Saturday, and I've already signed you up as a contestant."

"You're running away?" Delaney says incredulously when I call her later that night to tell her about my decision to go AWOL.

"No. I'm returning to my life," I answer calmly. "Calling it 'running away' makes it sound like I'm going to live in the streets and be a prostitute or something."

"But couldn't you get in big trouble for that? I thought the judge said she could send you to reform school or something."

"What else am I supposed to do?" I cry. "Sit around here and wait to be crowned rodent queen and then dunked in some nasty river? Besides, once I'm back in L.A., I'll find an attorney who can help me. Someone other than Luke."

"Good point," she concedes. "But how are you going to do it? Logistically speaking, I mean."

After pulling the Care Bears over my head for soundproofing, I give her a quick rundown of the plan, which basically has three steps: (1) I meet Sophie just before dawn Saturday morning; (2) Sophie drives me to the airport; and (3) I catch a plane. I know that doesn't exactly make for an exciting escape story, but I don't have time to do something daring like hitchhike across the country (not that I would, hello—can you say serial killers?), and there seems to be a shortage of knights on white horses, so I guess I'll just have to settle for Sophie and American Airlines.

With Delaney apprised of my comings and goings (emphasis on the *goings*) I drift off to sleep with a smile on my lips. All I have to do now is bide my time.

20
A Royal Homecoming

After I make up my mind to ditch Possum Grape for good, the rest of the week passes by in a blur. And before I really even have time to think about it, it's Saturday. I worried I might have a hard time sneaking out to meet Sophie, but it turns out to be surprisingly easy, thanks to Loretta Brown's hay barn catching on fire on the morning of my Big Escape. Poor Loretta. Apparently her nine-year-old twin grandsons decided to sneak a couple of cigarettes and—POOF!

Don't worry: Nobody was hurt except for the hay and the barn and probably the boys' backsides, assuming their parents go for the whole corporal punishment thing. Anyway, the entire family rushed over to help the volunteer fire department, so Sophie is able to drive right up to the front door and pick me up.

We manage to keep things cheery during the three-hour drive, but as soon as we enter short-term parking, Sophie gets misty. "I'm going to miss you," she sniffs, dabbing at her eyes with a crumpled napkin.

I pat her on the shoulder. "I'll miss you, too." As the words leave my mouth, I'm startled to realize that they're true. I really AM going to miss Sophie. And Dakota, too. *And Steven,* adds a little voice in the back of my head.

She throws the napkin on the floor and gives me a determined smile. "Will you call me as soon as the show is over? I want to hear all the details."

"Of course," I promise, leaning over to give her a hug. Then I step out of Buggy and head inside the airport and back to my old life.

When the plane lands in L.A., my first thought is that I am SO glad a long, black limousine is waiting for me instead of a mini-van, or—no offense to Sophie—a VW convertible. Even though I love her, I am definitely ready for a more luxurious mode of transportation than Buggy.

As soon as I pour a glass of sparkling water and settle myself against the soft leather of the limo's backseat, I instruct the driver to take me to Delaney's. I'd love to go to my house, but that would be, like, total suicide because José would have me on the first plane back to Possum Grape as soon as I stepped on the premises.

Delaney throws open the front door before I've even tipped the limo driver. "Yay! You're finally here!" She skips down the steps toward the car, but before we can do reunion hugs and air kisses, Tristan sweeps out the front door, followed by a guy with a video camera. Although Tristan always dresses very Vegas showgirl, he's obviously decided to take his wardrobe to the next level for television because in addition to his black spandex leggings and feathered halter top, he's also wearing a glittering white cape and diamond tiara.

"Darlings!" he exclaims as Delaney leans over to buss my cheek. "We have no time for kissy-kissy. We must work!" He claps his hands together. "Come."

Delaney rolls her eyes. "He's been acting like this all day. I think the Style network thing has gone to his head."

I smile as Tristan's cape whips the unsuspecting cameraman in the head as he whirls around to go back inside. Dorothy was SO right. There really is no place like home.

We follow Tristan and his cape obediently through the house toward the backyard, where tonight's festivities are taking place. The cameraman trails behind me and Delaney, taping everything, which, quite frankly, creeps me out. Call me crazy, but I think it's weird to have some guy following you around with a camera when you're just doing normal stuff. I'd never survive on a reality show. Except *Project Runway*. I'd totally kick you-know-what on that.

"Have you seen it?" I ask Delaney as we scamper after Tristan.

"What do you think I've been doing all day?" She laughs. "Tristan got here at, like, seven this morning. I opened the door without a stitch of makeup on and he turned that freaking camera on me." She frowns at me. "Why are you scratching like that? Is your skin dry or something?"

I yank my hand away from my stomach, which until half a second ago I didn't realize I was scratching through my shirt. Even though it's been a week since the chigger incident, my bites show no signs of improving. "No. I just, er, had an allergic reaction to some lotion." There are some things you can't tell even your best friend—like that invisible bugs are under your skin. "So what does it look like?" I persist, trying to ignore the insane itching that has just started on the back of my leg.

As the god of party planning, Tristan reserves the right to change anything and everything at his discretion, so I have no idea what might greet me when we step onto the veranda.

She smiles coyly. "You'll see." She pushes me toward Tristan, who has stopped in front of the wall of French doors that lead into the backyard. Before I get the chance to see anything through the glass, he slaps his hand over my eyes like a blindfold and propels me outside.

We go several steps before he brings me to a halt. "Voilà!" he cries, ripping his hand away.

I blink, trying to take in the scene in front of me. Once again, Tristan has proved that he's a genius. He's transformed the entire area into a kind of open-air living room. Hot pink couches accented with zebra throws and chic, wrought-iron chairs are grouped around dainty end tables while vintage chandeliers dangle elegantly from the low branches of trees. Stemless white roses float gracefully on the surface of the lagoon-shaped swimming pool that is filled with rose-tinted water. At the far end of the yard, men in construction garb are putting the finishing touches on the catwalk, which is stark white with black trim, exactly as I'd instructed.

I throw my arms around Tristan. "It's fabulous," I tell him, trying to ignore the cameraman who has moved in for a close-up.

Tristan, on the other hand, obviously loves having his every move filmed. He drags us around, pointing out every minute detail for the benefit of the camera.

By the time we finally escape to Delaney's bedroom, we only have a few hours to get ready. On the one hand, being on a tight schedule is good since I won't have time to get super nervous. But on the *other* hand, it also doesn't leave me much time to find something to wear. Although I entrusted Delaney with all the clothes for the fashion show—including the teeny-tiny Zane Porter minidress for myself—before I left for Possum Grape, that was before I had a million plus bug bites covering the lower half of my body. Now there's no way I can wear the Zane—unless, of course, I don't mind everyone thinking I have leprosy.

I think longingly of the bedroom that serves as my closet at home and the racks of dresses just waiting for me. If I could just slip inside . . . No. I shake my head. I can't risk José catching me. Delaney has a lot of great dresses, but thanks to our five-inch height difference, raiding her closet isn't an option either. And there's no time to go shopping because Andre will be here in less than an hour to do our hair and makeup. I sigh. That only leaves one option: a stylist.

Resigned, I flip open my cell phone and dial Zoe Riser's number. Zoe is a stylist I'm friends with. Normally I abhor the thought of using a stylist, but this is one of those instances where it can't be helped. I mean, don't get me wrong—stylists are great for super busy celebrities or for people who have no taste. But the few times I've used one I felt like I was cheating or something.

Zoe picks up on the third ring. "Hello," she yells into the phone. In the background is the loud thrum of rock music, which means she's probably on a video shoot.

"Zoe, it's West," I say loudly. "I need a favor."

"West?" she shouts back. "Hang on. I'm going to move so I can hear." I hear her say something unintelligible to someone around her and then the sound of a door closing. A few seconds later, the rock music becomes a muffled thumping.

"Sorry about that," Zoe says breathlessly. "I'm doing Bluestar's new video."

"How's it going?"

"Okay, except the bass player insisted on wearing this hideous shirt his girlfriend bought him."

"You couldn't talk him out of it?" I say sympathetically.

"Nope. He brought his girlfriend with him. Hey—" she breaks off. "I thought you were overseas or something."

"I just got back," I lie.

"Oh. So what's up?" Even though Zoe and I are friendly, we're not *that* friendly. She knows I must want something if I'm calling her.

"I know it's short notice, but I was hoping you could find me a dress for a party tonight."

Zoe immediately turns businesslike. "What kind of dress? Evening gown, cocktail, club dress, sundress?"

"Not an evening gown. Just something fun. But it has to be long," I add quickly. "Down to my ankles."

If Zoe thinks an ankle-length dress is a strange request, she doesn't show it. "What time do you need it?" she asks briskly.

"Like, in an hour?" I say tentatively.

"An *hour*?" She temporarily forgets her business persona. "Geez, West, I'm not a magician, here."

"That's just when I'm getting hair and makeup," I say quickly. "It can be later than that."

"I don't know. That's not much time, and I still have the video sh—"

"I'll pay extra," I interject. "Double, triple—whatever you want."

The offer of more money does the trick. "Okay," she concedes. "The shoots almost over, anyway. Tell me where I'm supposed to bring this fun, ankle-length dress."

21
The Party

"*Vous amusiez-vous bien à Paris?*"

I blink at my friend McKenzie, wondering why the hell she's speaking to me in some other language. She smiles patiently and persists with her strange behavior. "*Vous avez passé des bons vacances à Paris?*"

Delaney nudges me with the toe of her Jimmy Choo leopard slingbacks and says pointedly, "I think Kenzie is wondering about your trip, West."

For a horrified second I think Delaney is suggesting I tell Kenzie about Possum Grape, but then I remember my whole Paris/French immersion–school thing. Damn. I keep forgetting that everyone except Delaney thinks I've been in Paris. And of course it has to be Miss Fluent-in-Five-Languages-Because-My-Dad-Is-a-Fancy-Diplomat who reminds me. In French.

"Uh, *très bien*," I tell Kenzie, which is pretty much the extent of my grasp of the French language.

"Est-ce que votre grand-mère va bien?" she replies, leaving me no choice but to flee from her immediate, French-speaking vicinity. "I'm SO sorry, Kenz," I say, feigning sudden alarm. "But I just remembered that Delaney and I are supposed to check on something at the, er, bar. We'll talk Paris later, okay?" Without waiting for McKenzie to reply (in French, I'm sure), I grab Delaney by the arm and start pulling her through the crowd.

"Man, she SO almost busted you," Delaney says, laughing.

"I know!" I exclaim, glancing back over my shoulder to make sure McKenzie isn't following us.

Even though I was totally lying about having to check on something at the bar (duh), Delaney and I make a show of going over there, just in case McKenzie is watching. Plus, the bartender is an underwear model. That's one of the fringe benefits of having Tristan as your party planner—you're practically guaranteed a waitstaff of gorgeous, beefy guys.

"Hello, ladies." Mr. Bartender-Underwear model flashes a smile that shows off the perfect dimple in his cheek before handing me and Delaney each a pink-colored drink. In keeping with the pink theme of the party, Tristan has ordered Tabtinis as the drink of the evening, a rose-colored concoction of Tab Energy and vodka.

"Hi," we giggle in unison. We flirt shamelessly for a few minutes, then move over beside the illuminated pool to drink our Tabtinis and admire the fruits of our labor.

Well, technically it was Tristan's labor, but whatever. We're paying him, so we should get some of the credit, right?

"This is our best party ever," Delaney declares, sipping her drink as she surveys the scene around us.

"Absolutely," I murmur, following her gaze and trying desperately not to think about how good it would feel to hike my dress up and scratch the back of my legs until the skin bleeds. Delaney's right: It IS our best party ever. I mean, our parties always attract cool people, but this year is even better than normal. Delaney's backyard looks like the gathering place for a mandatory meeting of everyone who is young and hot in Hollywood.

"And we look adorable," Delaney adds, bumping her hip against mine.

Once again, she's right: We DO look adorable. Despite Zoe's claim that she's not a magician, she showed up less than an hour after I called, bearing a gorgeous, floor-length Dolce & Gabbana dress in lippi cat print, which is kind of like a miniature leopard print. Even though it's long, the skirt is a breezy, flowing type of thing, so it doesn't look too formal, and the top is strapless, so I don't look too covered up. And with the addition of a bronze cuff, some dangly earrings, and a quick air-brush tan by the makeup chick, I look pretty fabulous, if I do say so myself.

Delaney looks fab too. She was going to wear this purple Vera Wang fringed cocktail dress, which would have been cute, but once I saw what Zoe had brought, I convinced her to switch to a white Prada shift and accessorize it with this Yves Saint Laurent leopard belt I found in the back of her closet and her leopard Jimmy Choos. You know—so we'd have kind of a coordinated animal-print thing going on. Coordinated, but not too matchy-matchy. It turned out really well, too because we've been getting compliments all night, and not the fake kind.

"Doesn't Zane look hot?" I comment as I suddenly catch sight of the back of his chicly shabby blond mane.

Delaney nods. "Super hot. I love his new highlights."

I sigh wistfully. "I know. They look so natural." There's a moment of silence as we both contemplate the genius of Zane's hairdresser, and then Delaney says, "I think we should go ahead and do the fashion show."

"But the show is supposed to be the grand finale," I protest, dragging my eyes away from Zane's golden mane.

"Everybody's going to be totally smashed by then. I already saw Rachel passing out party favors."

"I thought Rachel was in rehab."

"She got out early," Delaney informs me, draining the last of her Tabtini. "Time off for good behavior."

"More like time off for screwing somebody in charge, I bet," I say dryly. In addition to being an addict, Rachel is also a total slut.

"Probably." Delaney laughs. "Still, we can't exactly kick her out of the party. So what do you think? Should we go ahead and do the show now?"

"I guess." I sigh, bummed. I was hoping to spend some time alone with Zane before I had to get down to business. Between my hostess duties and the, like, hundred or so people vying for his attention, we've hardly been able to say two words to each other. He DID give me a really sweet kiss when he got here, though. I could feel the girls around us mentally taking off their Manolos and stabbing me with them. BUT, I don't want the whole party to be in a chemically induced stupor during my show either, so after I finish my Tabtini, Delaney and I start rounding up the models.

It's no easy task since half of them are making out with the cast of *Entourage* and the other half are flitting around Justin Timberlake, but somehow we finally manage to corral them all into the backstage part of the temporary runway Tristan's crew has constructed.

Being backstage at a fashion show sounds really cool, but trust me, it's totally not. The stylists are bitchy, the models are moody, and the designer is always running around acting like a tyrant. All of those things are true at my show too, except for the tyrant part. I am *très* sweet to everyone.

"Are you nervous?" Delaney asks me as we huddle near the curtain that opens onto the catwalk, waiting for Tristan to cue the catchy club music I selected weeks ago.

I lift one shoulder in what I hope looks like a careless gesture. "A little." In reality, I'm practically shaking, but that's not the sort of thing I'd admit to anyone, even Delaney.

Finally, Tristan blasts the music and Delaney and I start shooing the models through the curtain. Delaney flashes me the thumbs-up sign as the first girl strikes a haughty pose at the end of the catwalk and a volley of applause erupts. "So far, so good."

The line of models continues strutting out and though

everything seems to be going well based on the sounds coming from the audience, I'm dying to get a look at Zane's face. Finally, I can't stand it any longer.

"Can you handle this?" I ask Delaney, speaking loudly so she can hear me over the music. "I want to find Zane."

She nods and gives me the thumbs-up sign again. I check my hair in one of the mirrors Tristan set up for the models and then hurry out into the audience to find Zane, my nerves humming with excitement. I can't wait to see how thrilled he is about my designs. He must be totally flipping out right now.

I scan the crush of people, looking for Zane's highlights, but after several seconds, I still haven't spotted the familiar blond streaks. Starting to feel anxious, I glance up at the catwalk. The show is nearly over; there are only a handful of models left until the grand finale, an ice-blue evening gown that took me almost three months to get to drape exactly right.

I give a sigh of relief as I recognize the form of Zane's bitchy assistant, Samantha, standing a few feet in front of me. She rarely lets him out of her sight, so he must be somewhere close by. I slide through the people between us and tap her on the shoulder. "Have you seen Zane?"

"Why?" she asks in a bored voice, not even giving me so much as a glance. Did I mention that she's a bitch?

"Because I need to talk to him."

She finally looks, or rather smirks, at me. "Sorry. He left."

"What do you mean he left?"

"I mean he left," she says sarcastically. "You know, that's when somebody gets in a car and drives away?"

"How long ago?" I demand, too panicked to think of an appropriately scathing retort.

She gives a condescending sniff. "I don't know, a couple of minutes ago, probably. I didn't have a stopwatch on him."

She calls after me with what I'm sure is another bitchy comment, but I'm already pushing my way through the crowd. If Zane really just left, I should be able to catch him before the valet brings his car around. I pause by the pool to slip off my shoes and run barefoot around to the front of the house.

My heart catches as I come around the corner and see Zane standing in the middle of the circular drive. His hands are shoved into the pockets of his faded corduroys and he's tapping his foot, looking impatient.

"Zane!"

He glances around at the sound of his name and breaks into a wide grin when he sees me coming toward him. "Hey, sweetie." He takes his hands out of his pockets and comes forward to meet me, pulling me against him so that his crotch is pressed against me. "That was some party you threw." He slides his hand down my back and squeezes my right buttock. "Too bad we didn't get to see more of each other."

Even though I'm pretty sure I already know the answer, I ask him the question anyway. "Did you see any of my show?"

He laughs and kisses me on the forehead. "Yeah, babe. It was great." He brings his face down lower and nuzzles against my neck. "Why don't you blow off the rest of this shindig and come back to my place? I promise to make it worth your while."

"What did you think about it?" I say stiffly, repressing the urge to shiver as he begins trailing kisses along the curve of my shoulder.

"What did I think about what?" he murmurs, moving back up my shoulder and starting across my collarbone.

"The show. What did you think about it?"

He stops the sensuous movement of his lips and lifts his head. "What was I supposed to think about?" he asks, giving me an amused look.

I push roughly against his chest, thrusting him away from me. "Oh, I don't know—maybe that it was good?"

"I already told you it was good."

"But what did you *think* about it?" I persist.

He swipes his hand through his highlights. "Look, I don't know what you want me to say here, babe."

"I want you to say that I'm good," I blurt. "That you want me to be your intern next summer."

He lets out a burst of laughter. "My intern? Babe, no offense, but did you do an extra one of those party favors your friend was passing out?"

"You didn't even watch it, did you?" I say accusingly. "Why did you even come?"

He narrows his eyes. "I came here to network and because I thought you wanted to have some fun," he says meanly. "Not to watch some pitiful fashion show put on by a teenager who thinks just because she wears couture she can design it."

I'm sure that at some point in the future I'll be curled up in the fetal position, crying over the awful, horrendous thing that just came out of his mouth, but right now, I just want to scratch his eyes out. And if I wasn't pretty sure that's considered, like, assault or battery or something, I would. Instead, I say scathingly, "Well, I guess we have a lot in common, then, because according to *Women's Wear Daily*, you can't design it either. What was it they said about your work?" I tap my finger against my cheek, pretending to think. "Oh yeah — 'uninspired and vaguely comical.'"

The color drains out of his face as he stares at me, stunned. It's a low blow on my part because I'm quoting what *WWD* said about his very first collection a few years ago, before he became a "star." Since then, they've totally praised him, but I KNEW that criticism would still sting him.

"What's wrong, Zane? Are you surprised a pitiful teenager like me knows how to read?" My words are punctuated by the hum of an engine as the valet brings Zane's silver convertible to a smooth stop in front of us.

At the sight of his car, Zane seems to snap back to his senses. He looks at me as the valet hurriedly scrambles out of the driver's seat. "*WWD* doesn't know shit, and neither do you. You're just a spoiled rich girl whose father is a crook."

I launch myself at him, the assault-and-battery thing no longer a concern. But before I can cause him bodily harm, he shoves a twenty-dollar bill at the valet and slides into the driver's seat of the convertible. A half second later, the convertible shoots forward.

Enraged, I pull back my arm and hurl my left heel at it with all my might. It grazes the convertible's back end and tumbles to the ground. I lift my arm to throw the right one, but the sight of my poor, mistreated shoe lying forlornly on its side in the middle of the driveway stops me. OMG, I have to get control of myself, I realize, shocked by my own behavior. I'm throwing high-end footwear at a moving vehicle.

I quickly glance around to see if there are any witnesses to my shameful behavior. The valet is watching me warily, waiting to see if I'm going to flip out even further. I smile at him so he'll know I'm not dangerous, but that only makes him look more scared. I sigh. Who can blame him? I make a mental note to give all the valets a bonus.

Even though my festive mood is beyond dead, I have no choice but to go back to the party and pretend like everything's fine. A hostess can't exactly bail on her own party. Plus, Zane's bitch assistant will no doubt give him a full report on everything that happened after he left and there's NO WAY I'm going to give him the satisfaction of thinking he upset me so much, I couldn't go back to the party. Because I'm not upset. I'm fine. I'm better than fine, actually; I'm great. And after I repeat that to myself a few thousand times, maybe it will really be true.

22
Sometimes Humiliation Is a Good Thing

"You can't stay in bed forever." Delaney's reasonable tone of voice sounds frighteningly like Alice's.

"Why not?" My voice is muffled because of the pillow over my face. Remember how I said that at some point I'd be curled up in the fetal position? Yeah, I was right.

"For starters, this is MY bed."

I yank the pillow off and stare up at her incredulously. "You're begrudging me your bed in my time of need?"

"Second," she continues, ignoring me, "you're being a drama queen."

"Hmmph." I'm not even dignifying that with a response. My dreams just got crushed into a million tiny little pieces. If she thinks calling me a drama queen is going to get me out of this bed, she's smoking crack.

Then she pulls out the big guns. "And third, Blanca says she's not making you any more chocolate frosting."

"She wouldn't," I gasp, shooting up into a sitting position. Delaney's housekeeper's frosting is, like, the only thing keeping me from slitting my wrists.

Delaney smiles, pleased she's finally gotten my attention. "She would. Actually, she said she's not bringing you anything else until you take a shower and come downstairs."

"But that's just"—I search for the appropriate word—"evil."

"Alice would call it 'tough love.'"

I flop back against the pillows. "Fuck Alice."

Delaney sits on the edge of the bed. "Just get up," she cajoles. "We'll go to Fred Segal. You'll feel so much better."

I shake my head. "This is way beyond the powers of retail therapy. I think I'm scarred for life."

"Don't be silly," Delaney says, reminding me of Dakota. "Shopping cures everything—except, like, cancer." She reaches forward and grasps the duvet.

"I'm serious," I say stubbornly, clutching it so she can't pull it off me. "I'm not getting out of bed. Ever."

Her voice turns stern. "You're being ridiculous." She yanks on the duvet, but now I have both hands on it, gripping it for all I'm worth.

She jerks harder. "Let go."

"No."

We continue playing tug-of-war until finally Delaney throws up her hands. "Fine," she says disgustedly. "Stay there forever, if you want. I'm going shopping."

I watch her flounce out of the room and I smile to myself. I KNEW she'd give up. Even though we have the same trainer, I have WAY more upper-body strength than she does. I only enjoy my pitiful victory for about two seconds, though, because then I remember that mean, evil Blanca has cut off my food supply. I suppose she thinks she's all clever and stuff, trying to use hunger to force me out of bed. *Well, I'll show her,* I vow silently, pulling the duvet over my head. *I'll just lie here and starve to death.*

I maintain my hunger strike until late that afternoon, when the big, juicy In-N-Out burger that appears behind my lids every time I close my eyes finally forces me to admit defeat and emerge from my haven. Plus, I seriously have to pee.

I pad into Delaney's bathroom, wincing as I catch sight of my reflection in the mirror. Not only do I feel like shit, I look like it too. No wonder Delaney is so worried about me. I look like Courtney Love. Hibernating in bed wearing a dress and full makeup is not a good idea.

After I pee, I strip out of the dress and rummage around in Delaney's vanity for makeup remover. Even though I've decided to spend the rest of my life as a hermit, I don't want to be a hermit with clogged pores.

As I'm dabbing at my eyes with a cotton ball (you should never, ever scrub—it causes wrinkles), I hear my cell phone trill in the bedroom. It's rung, like, a thousand times today, but I haven't picked up, partly because I don't feel like talking to anybody and partly because I'm pretty sure a bunch of those calls were from Sherri. And I REALLY don't feel like talking to her.

I don't care what that stupid judge ordered. I am not going back to Possum Grape. Ever. They can't make me. I'm going to be a hermit with clear skin right here in L.A. As soon I get an In-N-Out burger.

I'm in Delaney's closet perusing her new collection of Juicy to see if there's anything I can fit into when I remember my promise to Sophie at the airport. Crap. I'd told her I'd call her as soon as the show was over and tell her how it went. And she was so excited for me, she's probably been, like, sitting by the phone since yesterday.

For a moment I consider blowing her off, anyway, but my conscience won't let me. Sophie WAS super nice to me (after we got over the whole Jaci thing). It's not her fault my life is over.

Leaving the closet, I snag my cell phone off Delaney's dresser and dial Sophie's number. She answers before the end of the first ring, and I stifle a groan. Great. She really WAS waiting by the phone.

"Where have you been?" she cries. "I've been trying to call you all day."

Ooops. I guess some of those calls today were from her. "I'm so sorry, Soph. It's just that—"

"You're never going to believe what happened this morning," she rushes on breathlessly, cutting me off.

My stomach clenches guiltily. Oh, no—what if Sherri found out Sophie took me to the airport and went over to her house or something? Sophie has been SO nice. I would feel awful if she got grounded or something because of me, especially since it turned out to be all for nothing.

Sophie's voice becomes a high-pitched squeal. "Tori Diaz called the shop! Looking for you!" She starts speaking so rapidly, I can barely understand her. "Jaci didn't know either of our cell numbers—I mean, why would she since she's a total bitch—but she told her the name of my mom's store and then Tori got the number from information. And then she called! This morning! Can you believe it?" she finishes.

Great. My life is in shambles, and now Sophie is flipping out. Oh, well. At least I don't have to tell her about Zane right away. "I have no idea what you're talking about," I say calmly.

"Didn't you hear me? Tori Diaz called the store. Looking for you!"

"Who is Tori Diaz?"

"Tori Diaz," Sophie repeats, as if saying it again is somehow going to make me less clueless. "You know—the fashion designer. She lives in Dallas."

"Never heard of her." *And I don't want to,* I add silently. My fashion days are SO over. Besides, what kind of fashion designer lives in *Texas*? She probably dresses, like, rodeo queens or something.

"Really?" Sophie sounds surprised. "She's super successful. Anyway, she saw Jaci wearing the Masterpiece and she loved it. She wants to know if you want to sell it in her boutique."

"Sophie, the Masterpiece was hideous. We wanted Jaci to look *awful*, not good. Remember?"

"I know," Sophie says happily. "It totally backfired on us."

"But she *did* look awful," I remind her. "So why would I want anything to do with this Tori person when she obviously has bad taste?"

"Because she's known for promoting new talent," Sophie replies. "She showcases young and upcoming designers in her store. You know—to help them get a following."

Yeah. If this chick loves the Masterpiece, I can just IMAG-INE what kind of talent she's showcasing in her store. "Look, Soph, I'm glad she likes it and everything, but I'm through with designing." The only way to make her understand is to tell her about last night, so I take a deep breath and give her all the gory details.

"So?" she says when I finish.

"So, my fashion career is over. Weren't you listening?"

"You're throwing in the towel just because some jerk was more interested in your body than your designs?" She sounds incredulous and pissed at the same time.

Man, what does a girl have to do to get a little bit of sym-pathy around this place? First Delaney and Blanca are hard-asses, and now Sophie is going all after-school-special on me. "Zane isn't just some jerk," I say defensively. "He's THE hottest designer in fashion."

"He's the hottest designer *right now*. They'll be somebody hotter in six months, probably less."

"You don't understand. I can't do it anymore. I'm tired. I'm finished." *I'm humiliated*. I blink, startled at the admission my subconscious just tossed into the forefront of my brain. I've felt a lot of things since last night—angry, depressed, sad—but up until now, it didn't occur to me that I was *embarrassed* about what happened. I mean, I know that would probably seem like a "duh" thing to most people, but when you're rich, beautiful, and have great style, you don't exactly have too many occasions to feel embarrassed, you know?

But that's exactly what I am, I realize uncomfortably. I'm embarrassed. Humiliated, mortified, disgraced. All three put together. And that is COMPLETELY unacceptable.

I set my jaw into a determined line and ask Sophie the question she's been waiting for me to ask the entire phone call: "What's this Tori person's number?"

23
My New Life

"Not the blue ones, the pink." My words are muffled because of the pins in my mouth.

"These?"

I nod as Kate finally plucks the correct box of beads from the mess on the table. She comes over and places the box by my elbow. "How long is that going to take?" she asks, frowning down at the miniskirt to which I'm gluing rhinestones.

"Not long. I have to mail everything tomorrow so Tori will get it before the weekend."

"I'm almost finished with these," Sophie informs us, gesturing to the pile of neatly folded shirts next to her sewing machine.

"It's about time," Kate mutters. "She's been working on those stupid things forever."

Okay. I know you're dying to hear about the details that led up to this scene of harmonious interaction between me, Sophie, and Kate, so I'll give you a recap. But it has to be quick because

Steven is picking me up in twenty minutes. Don't freak out! I'll get to that part in a sec.

So, after I hung up with Sophie that day, I called Tori who, FYI, is this totally cool woman in her midthirties who just started designing about three years ago. And Sophie was right about her being super successful: Apparently her boutique in Dallas is MAJORLY popular with the girls down there. I feel totally guilty for being so judgmental about her address. It turns out she's never even *been* to a rodeo.

Anyway, in the middle of Tori telling me about her clothes and her store and asking about my designs, I realized that God was trying to do that whole opening-a-window thing. You know—since He slammed the door in my face with Zane and all. And since I'm hardly qualified to argue with the Supreme Ruler of the Universe, when Tori asked me if I would send her some of my work, I said absolutely.

The rest, as they say, is history. Tori liked my designs and offered to sell them in her store. Sophie was right about her helping young designers. She's totally awesome. So now I'm a "real" fashion designer, except I can't take all the credit for my new success because there's no way I could do all this without Sophie and Kate's help. Yes, even Kate, little ray of sunshine that she is. She's actually acted fairly decent about the whole deal. Of course, I'm paying her, so that helps.

You've probably figured out by now that I'm back in Possum Grape, which, I have to admit, I'm not exactly thrilled about. Sherri's still being all military about the whole living-with-my-family thing. And Daddy's appeal just got denied, so it looks like I'm stuck—for now, at least. Delaney is still pretty upset about our new long-distance friendship, but Sherri said she could come for a visit during spring break. I can't WAIT to see Delaney's face when we pick her up at the airport in the minivan.

As for Steven, it's not polite to kiss and tell, so I can't share the REALLY juicy stuff, but I will tell you this: He's a really, really sweet guy. As soon as I got back to Possum Grape, I realized how stupid I was for not taking advantage of what was right in front of me. And I'm SO glad things didn't work out with Zane (especially that one particular thing). Because Steven is a WAY better person than Zane ever thought about being. And when he calls me Princess, I feel like the most beautiful, special girl in the world.

And last, I no longer have a Big Dirty Secret. But like I said, it's not polite to kiss and tell, so I guess you'll just have to use your imagination for that part.

Oh, and if you're ever in Dallas, be sure to drop by the store and buy one of our bestselling Possum Queen T-shirts. They're all the rage.

About the Author

Julie Linker was born and raised in Arkansas, where she still lives with her husband and little girl. Unlike West, she loves living in the South and has no desire to move to Beverly Hills (although she wouldn't mind a shopping trip on Rodeo Drive). To find out more about Julie, visit her website at www.julielinker.com.

From bestselling author
KATE BRIAN

♥ ♥ ♥ ♥ ♥

Juicy reads for the **sweet** and the **sassy!**

Lucky T
"Fans of Meg Cabot's *The Princess Diaries* will enjoy it." —*SLJ*

Megan Meade's Guide to the McGowan Boys
Featured in *Teen* magazine!

The Virginity Club
"*Sex and the City: High School Edition.*" —*KLIATT*

The Princess & the Pauper
"Truly exceptional chick-lit." —*Kirkus Reviews*

FROM SIMON PULSE
♥ Published by Simon & Schuster ♥

THE WORD IS OUT!

melissa de la cruz

IS THE AUTHOR EVERYONE'S CHATTING ABOUT.

♥♠ WANTED ♦♣

Single Teen Reader in search of a FUN romantic comedy read!

How NOT to Spend Your Senior Year
CAMERON DOKEY

Royally Jacked
NIKI BURNHAM

Ripped at the Seams
NANCY KRULIK

Cupidity
CAROLINE GOODE

Spin Control
NIKI BURNHAM

South Beach Sizzle
SUZANNE WEYN & DIANA GONZALEZ

She's Got the Beat
NANCY KRULIK

30 Guys in 30 Days
MICOL OSTOW

Animal Attraction
JAMIE PONTI

A Novel Idea
AIMEE FRIEDMAN

Scary Beautiful
NIKI BURNHAM

Getting to Third Date
KELLY McCLYMER

Dancing Queen
ERIN DOWNING

Major Crush
JENNIFER ECHOLS

Do-Over
NIKI BURNHAM

Love Undercover
JO EDWARDS

Prom Crashers
ERIN DOWNING

Gettin' Lucky
MICOL OSTOW

The Boys Next Door
JENNIFER ECHOLS

In the Stars
STACIA DEUTSCH & RHODY COHON

Available from Simon Pulse ♥♠ Published by Simon & Schuster

Get smitten with these sweet & sassy British treats:

Prada Princesses
by Jasmine Oliver

Three friends tackle
the high-stakes world
of fashion school.

10 Ways to Cope with Boys
by Caroline Plaisted

What every girl *really*
needs to know.

Ella Mental
by Amber Deckers

If only every girl had a
"Good Sense" guide!

From Simon Pulse · Published by Simon & Schuster

Public Displays
of
Confession

Like a guilty-pleasure celeb magazine, these juicy Hollywood stories will suck you right in. . . .

Did you **love** this book?

Want to get the
hottest books **free**?

Log on to
www.SimonSaysTEEN.com
to find out how you can get
free books from **Simon Pulse**
and become part of our **IT Board**,
where you can tell **US**, what **you** think!

SIMON
PULSE